OPERATOR 5:
RAIDERS OF THE RED DEATH

SECRET SERVICE #5 ™
OPERATOR 5
AMERICA'S UNDERCOVER ACE

RAIDERS OF
THE RED DEATH

By Curtis Steele

STEEGER BOOKS • 2020

CHAPTER 1
FIELD OFFICE #3

NERO FIDDLED while Rome burned. And nearly two thousand years later, in the City of Washington, D.C., distinguished guests at the brilliant reception given by Mrs. Glenna Hawkins, dances to soft music and chatted idly of trivial things. And even while they laughed and chatted, newspapers were being hawked in the streets; newspapers carrying strange, black, disturbing headlines:

AZTEC REVOLUTION OVERTURNS MEXICAN GOVERNMENT! SELF-STYLED DESCENDANT OF MONTEZUMA MAKES SELF EMPEROR!

The voices crying extras did not penetrate to gay guests in the home of Mrs. Hawkins. Indeed, few except two of the guests concerned themselves much with what was happening in little Mexico. The two who were interested were none other than the American Secretaries of War and of State, whose limousines were conspicuous among those parked outside Mrs. Hawkins' home.

But those two gentlemen were not in evidence in the huge reception room, and the other guests naturally assumed that they were closeted somewhere, discussing weighty matters.

So the gay reception went on....

IN NEW YORK CITY, a furtive man slunk out of the

Times Square subway station, lingered a moment at the corner of Forty-second Street and Times Square, glancing behind him frequently as if he were fearful of being followed.

He was a thin man; his hands were small, almost effeminate. His face was long, his features sharp, pinched with some sort of inward terror. He belonged, obviously, to one of the Latin races.

His eyes strayed upward and across Forty-second Street, to

2

The horror of Montezuma's bursting death kept people in mortal fear!

the Times Building. There, high above the heads of the passing crowds, was the ingenious news strip consisting of an arrangement of electric light bulbs, by which the latest happenings all over the world were flashed before the eyes of passing New Yorkers. The electric-light bulbs carried the illuminated words clear around the building, and the effect was that of a continuous sentence which could be read by anyone walking on any side of the tall Times Building.

Now the thin man seemed to shiver as he read the moving sentence that flashed around:

AZTECS IN FULL CONTROL OF MEXICO... THEIR LEADER NAMES HIMSELF MONTEZUMA THE THIRD... DECLARES WAR AGAINST UNITED STATES... OUR PRESIDENT DECLARES THAT UNITED STATES TROOPS WILL CRUSH AZTECS WITHIN FORTY-EIGHT HOURS....

The little man shivered as he read, and mumbled to himself under his breath. He cast a last, backward glance at the subway kiosk from which he had emerged into the street, then suddenly made up his mind and turned to enter the drugstore on the corner.

Behind him in the street, passing New Yorkers were reading further news items on the Times Building:

THIRTEEN PERSONS REPORTED KILLED IN STRANGE EXPLOSIONS IN VARIOUS PARTS OF COUNTRY... THOUGHT TO BE WORK OF FOREIGN SABOTAGE AGENTS... METHOD OF BOMBINGS REMAINS A MYSTERY....

The little man did not see these last news flashes, because he was already in the drugstore, crouched at one of the telephone booths.

4

Had he not been so nervous, he might have noticed the man who had come out of the subway kiosk behind him, and who had slid into a convenient doorway while he himself hesitated at the corner. Now, the second man strolled casually past the drug-store, peered in, saw the other in the telephone booth. He walked by the drug-store entrance, disappeared down the street.

The thin man, meanwhile, had inserted his nickel in the slot, and dialed 211—the long distance operator. He asked for a number in Washington, D.C., and two minutes later he was speaking Viciously into the transmitter.

"Thees," he said cautiously, "ees Miguel Esprada. You—remember?"

"Yes!" a crisp voice at the other end answered. "Did you find out anything?"

The thin man glanced about him furtively, brought his mouth close to the instrument. "You 'eve promise' me that you weel pay ten thousan' dollar—"

"No," the voice at the other end broke in. "I promised you five thousand. Come, Esprada, I'm very busy. Have you five thousand dollars' worth of information for me?"

ESPRADA'S EYES gleamed with avarice. "I 'ave, señor. But I am in the very great danger. You mus' send two of your—w'at-you-call?—operators to meet me and take me to Washington. There I weel talk. I can tell you w'ere is the secret 'eadquarters of the Aztecs in New York. I can tell you 'ow they make the men to explode. But you must be careful. There is a leak in your War Department. The nephew of the Secretary—Vance—"

His voice broke in a thin shriek of terror as the air in the drug-store seemed suddenly to change. Customers and clerks turned at the note of terror in Esprada's voice. A hush suddenly descended upon the noisy interior of the store.

And through that hush rose Esprada's fear-chilled voice: "The exploding death! Help—"

He started to run for the door, and suddenly his panic was communicated to the throng in the store. A mad stampede began toward the street. Jerks hurdled counters, men and women pushed each other roughly out of the way. And Esprada raced faster than all.

But he was too late. Abruptly, as if a huge hand had reached out from infinity, all that throng in the brilliantly lit store ceased to run, staggered, fought against an overwhelming power that seemed to be pushing the eyeballs out of their heads, to be causing the blood to burst from their nostrils and their eardrums.

And then, each individual in that store seemed to *burst from within!*

With a terrific series of popping explosions, all those people in the store burst into torn and bloody fragments of flesh and bone and clothing—as if a time bomb inside them had exploded!

The air was filled with blood and the stench of burned flesh, with flying fragments of humanity. The electric lights shattered into bits, plunging the interior into darkness. The plate-glass windows of the store burst outwards in shards, catapulting bits of human flesh into the street. Not a soul was left alive in the store....

Outside, people fled from the scene of the sudden holocaust, shrieking in terror. Something dreadful, inexplicable, had

happened. The corner of Times Square
and Forty-second Street was transformed
abruptly from a busy, bustling intersection, into a charnel house.

HUITZILOPOCHTLI
AZTEC GOD of WAR

Police patrol cars raced toward
the scene with sirens screaming. Fire
trucks roared through the streets. Gas
and electric emergency squads arrived.
Police reserves established a wide cordon
about the corner, while other bluecoats
attempted to quell the near-panic of persons in the subway
system below who had heard the explosion.

Reporters sped to nearby telephones to rap out the dreadful
news to their papers, while high across the street, on the tall
Times Building, the news-strip continued to flash its items:

AZTECS REPORTED MOBILIZING TEXAS
BORDER... SPOKESMAN AT WHITE HOUSE STATES
THERE IS NO CAUSE FOR ALARM.

And the man who had been Miguel Esprada a few minutes
ago, was no more. Bits of him lay scattered on Times Square,
together with shreds of the other unfortunate patrons of that
store. The secrets he had offered to sell would never be sold....
IN WASHINGTON, a blue-eyed, keen-faced young man
jiggled the hook of his private telephone desperately.

"Operator!" he barked. "I was connected with New York.
Reestablish that connection at once. This is government business!"

7

"Sorry, sir," the operator answered. "New York reports that there has been an explosion in the store where the pay telephone was located. Everybody in the store was killed!"

"Thank you," the young man said in a low voice, and racked the receiver slowly. His blue eyes had become suddenly cloudy as he stared across his desk. After a moment, he picked up another telephone beside the one he had just used, spoke three words into it: "Field Office Three!"

A few seconds later he was saying: "Chief! Are the Secretary of State and the Secretary of War there yet? Insist that they wait. It's more serious than they realize. We *must* make them understand. Yes, I'll be there inside of ten minutes!"

He hung up, picked up the other telephone, and spoke a number into it. When he got his connection his voice, which had been crisp and tense, softened a bit.

"Tim? You dressed? Big doings on. I'll pick you up at the usual corner in five minutes. Don't keep me waiting!"

ON A side street in Washington, D.C., there is a down-at-heels two-story stucco building to which no one ever pays any attention. The small plot of ground in front of it is unkempt, full of weeds.

A faded "To Let" sign on the door directs any one interested to inquire at, a real estate office—not in Washington, but in New York City. Anyone desirous of renting this house would find his path beset by many difficulties. The rental demanded was so high as to deter any prospect from further inquiries. But should he be persistent enough to get in touch with the New York real estate firm; and should he be profligate enough to be willing to pay the exorbitant rental, he would then be informed that the owner had investigated his references and found them unsatisfactory. The house remained unkempt and apparently untenanted....

Around the corner from it was the home of Mrs. Glenna Hawkins, the popular Washington hostess. It was here that the splendid reception was being given this evening, and it was outside her home that the limousines of the Secretaries of State and of War were parked.

The affair was well on its way when additional guests arrived. A young man and a boy drove up in a long, low-slung roadster whose throttled purr spoke of great reserves of power.

Because of the press of cars on the block, these two parked at some distance up the street. The young man got out, revealing a tall, well-knit, athletic figure, faultlessly attired in evening clothes. He had keen, intelligent, blue eyes; a strong chin, and a virile mouth. He moved lithely, with poise and with the suggestion of swift efficiency in emergencies. He was Operator 5 of the American Intelligence. Only a few persons knew him as James Christopher.

The boy, a freckle-faced lad of perhaps fourteen or fifteen, remained in the car, he slipping behind the wheel into the seat just vacated by the young man. His youthful, mischievous gray eyes twinkled as he said:

"Not owning a tuxedo, Jimmy, I guess I'll have to stay out here with the other chauffeurs. When the party's over, bring me out some of Mrs. Hawkins' caviar sandwiches, will you?"

The young man whom he addressed as Jimmy, did not smile.

He glanced keenly up and down the street, his gaze probing into the shadows opposite, and on either side. He said grimly:

"It won't be that kind of a party, Tim. Now I'm sorry I called you. I hate to leave you out here."

Tim laughed, youthfully, infectiously. "It's not me they want, Jimmy. It's you. And besides, they couldn't get at me if they tried. You know darn well this car is bullet-proof; and with the windows up and the doors locked—"

The young man nodded, smiled affectionately. "All right, kid. As long as you're here, I can use you. Turn the window up as soon as I leave you, *and don't open it for anybody!* If you see Vance Snyder, the nephew of the Secretary of War, coming out, tail him and phone me as soon as you can. It's mighty important that we keep him in sight from now on!"

The boy's face suddenly grew serious. "Okay, Jimmy," he said quietly. "You can depend on me. And—good luck to you, Jimmy!"

The young man watched while Tim closed the window beside the driver's seat; then he turned silently and strode down the street toward the brilliantly lit home of Mrs. Glenna Hawkins.

As he walked, in swift, long, space-covering strides, his face—though that of a young man in the middle twenties—was etched in grim lines as if its owner had crammed many experiences into the short span of years. He walked swiftly, on the balls of his feet, hands swinging loosely at his sides. His appearance was deceptively casual, but his whole body was taut, ready to swing into blinding action at the first call of emergency....

At the door of the Hawkins home, he presented an engraved

invitation to the flunkey, who relieved him of his hat and topcoat and led him into the reception hall. The name on that card of invitation was: "Carleton Victor," and it was thus that the flunkey announced him.

Glenna Hawkins, the hostess, was surrounded by a bevy of admiring men as he approached her. She excused herself, and gave him her hand, smiling graciously.

"So very nice of you to come, Mr. Victor," she said in her soft, drawling Southern voice.

GLENNA HAWKINS was a vivacious little thing, full of nervous energy. Her full, rather plump figure was more than made up for by the sparkle in her lively eyes and by her constant stream of witty chatter. A widow at twenty-six, she had half of Washington offering to bestow another name upon her. Her husband, a career man in the diplomatic service, had died in an accident a couple of years before. Somehow, she seemed suddenly to have acquired unlimited funds, and her functions had become the talk of Washington.

She stood there now, holding the tall young man's hand, smiling and seeming to exchange trivial remarks with him. None of the guests were within earshot, for she had managed to move away from her admirers without appearing to do so. To any one observing her, it seemed that she was the perfect hostess, making her latest arrival feel at home. In reality, she was saying: "They are waiting for you, Operator 5. 7-7 is there, with the Secretaries of State and War. You'd better go right in to them before they get impatient. Use entrance number three. You know the way."

The young man who had been variously addressed that

JIMMY CHRISTOPHER

evening as "Jimmy," as "Carlton Victor," and as "Operator 5," smiled as if Glenna Hawkins had said something very amusing. He seemed to be entirely preoccupied with his charming hostess. But his eyes had already swept over the assembled company, had noted the presence of a certain man.

He spoke urgently now, swiftly, though he continued to smile in a pleasant, carefree way: "I see that Vance Snyder is here. Did he come with the Secretary of War, or did he come alone?"

Involuntarily Glenna Hawkins' eyes strayed across the room to the sallow-skinned, foppishly dressed man who stood by himself in the middle of the room, shunning the gay groups about him. This man was evidently suffering from some sort of nervous strain. His small, restless eyes had flicked many times toward the tall young man, and each time he had turned away quickly, as if he feared to be observed.

Glenna Hawkins replied to her guest's query: "Vance Snyder came alone, just a couple of minutes before you did. Why do you ask? Surely there can't be anything wrong about Vance; he's private secretary to the Secretary of War—as well as being his nephew!"

The young man smiled thinly. "I am afraid that Vance Snyder needs watching. Keep your eye on him when I leave you. If he should follow me out of here, give me the usual signal—two green lights in the passageway."

The hostess' eyes expressed concern, though her lips continued to smile for the benefit of anyone who might be watching. "But surely you don't suspect Vance Snyder? The Secretary's nephew—"

The young man shrugged. "Even the Secretary's nephew," he said. "There are strange things occurring these last few days. Men in positions of trust are becoming traitors—men in very high places. There is danger all about us. If I can only convince those two old fossils inside, before it's too late."

Quickly Glenna Hawkins put a hand on his arm. "Is—is it that serious, Operator 5? Is the country really in danger?"

He nodded somberly. "In very great danger, Mrs. Hawkins. We are faced by a very powerful menace—so great that it can corrupt men like the nephew of the Secretary of War!" Suddenly he bowed to her. "I had better go. We may be observed, and we've talked too long already. Remember, watch Vance Snyder."

He left her, and started across the gay reception room. The buzz of light conversation assailed his ears on all sides, but he did not smile. He wondered how these people would act if they

14

were suddenly made aware of the things that he had learned tonight. He could imagine the laughter dying on their lips, could almost see the dreadful fear growing in their eyes. But by no outward sign could anyone tell what was going on behind those quiet blue eyes of his. To all appearances he was a slightly bored society gentleman, aimlessly strolling across the room.

HIS EYES sought Vance Snyder, but found no trace of the man in the gay assemblage. The Secretary's nephew had apparently vanished….

Operator 5 threaded his way casually among the guests, bowing here and there to an acquaintance, but managing deftly not to engage in any lengthy conversations. Finally he reached the other end of the ballroom, stepped out into a corridor. He glanced both ways to be sure that he was not observed, then crossed and opened a door opposite.

He slipped into an unlighted room, closed the door behind him, and made his way across in the dark. His hand touched a knob, he opened another door, and entered a small closet. Here he used a small, flat flashlight that fitted inconspicuously in his evening clothes, directed its beam at the wall.

His long, dexterous fingers felt along the wall, counting a row of nail heads that ran across it at about the height of a man's head. When he reached the eighth, he pressed hard with his thumb, and a hidden spring clicked. The entire wall rose at his touch, revealing to the beam of his light, a narrow wooden staircase. Unhesitatingly, he started down, and as his foot touched the second step the wall descended behind him, closing off the closet.

When he reached the bottom of the flight of stairs, he followed a dank cellar wall for ten paces. Here he stooped and touched another spring. A section of the wall slid away, and he stepped through into a low tunnel. The wall closed behind him once more, and he followed the passageway for perhaps ten feet.

Suddenly he stopped, his eyes focused on two small green bulbs on the wall at his right which had begun to glow.

He pressed a button in token that he had seen the signal, and the light in the bulbs died once more. Using his flashlight, he hurried along the passageway for perhaps fifteen feet more, where it abruptly ended in a blank wall.

He bent down, focused his flashlight on a small hole in the wall, about two feet from the floor. At once there was a rumbling noise, and a section of the wall slid away, revealing a lighted room. He stepped within, and the wall-panel closed behind him.

A steady clack of typewriters greeted him from perhaps two dozen desks arranged in rows. At each of these desks, men in shirtsleeves worked. Behind the desks, other men worked at long rows of filing cabinets along the walls. The scene was one of bustling activity.

The men at the desks seemed to know him, for they nodded respectfully as he passed through the room into a small foyer-like space where a single man sat on guard. The man arose when he entered, smiled in welcome, said:

"You better hurry, Operator 5. Z-7 has sent down twice already to ask if you were here."

The young man did not smile. He asked swiftly: "Someone just came in through entrance number four. Who was it?"

The guard nodded. "Only Vance Snyder. He went upstairs, said he had an urgent message for his uncle. I didn't like to stop him. Did I do wrong?"

The young man nodded grimly. "I'm afraid you did, Sommers."

He left the bewildered guard, passed through two more rooms filled with busy men, and then up a flight of stairs to the upper floor.

HERE THERE was similar activity. The entire floor was divided into glass-enclosed rooms. In some of them were tele-typewriters, in others were batteries of phones. Everywhere men were working at top speed. At the places where the windows should be, long strips of soundproof board had been nailed. No light shone out of this house, no sound came from it. Huge exhaust fans carried the stale air away, and brought in fresh. In an alcove at the side of the hall was an electric stove upon which fresh coffee was constantly being brewed for the busy men.

And the faded "To Let" sign on the front door, the unkempt lawn, concealed the fact that here was housed a unit designated as WDC Field Office No. 3 of the United States Intelligence Service. The hostess in the house around the corner was a name in Washington society, but just another number in the rolls of the Intelligence Service. And she performed a highly useful duty in acting as a blind for Field Office No. 3.

Operator 5 hurried past the glass-enclosed offices, mounted to the second floor, and rapped twice at a door.

It was opened by a solidly built man whose flashing black eyes and black hair gave emphasis to his thin-lipped, shark featured face. He smiled, stood aside for Operator 5 to enter. His face now, even though he smiled, was lined with care. "We've been waiting for you, Operator 5," he said.

Operator 5 nodded to the Secretary of State and the Secretary of War, who were seated on either side of the polished mahogany desk in the center of the room. Then he turned to the man who had admitted him.

"I'm sorry, Chief," he said, "but I had to wait for an important phone call. Then, I had to double on the trail here, to make sure we weren't followed."

As he spoke, he fingered a watch-charm, fashioned in the shape of a death's-head, which hung on a chain across his vest. He gazed somberly at the three men. "Gentlemen!" he announced crisply, "I have very disturbing news for you!"

The Secretary of State, a stout man with a round, shrewd face and a thin scattering of gray hair, arose from the desk, frowning. "Your chief here tells me," he began irritably, "that you have been advancing some wild theories—"

"Wait, sir!" Operator 5 broke in. "My theories are far from wild. You, sir—and the whole nation, for that matter—are sitting on a keg of dynamite. And I am speaking literally now!"

The Secretary of State uttered a short, impatient laugh.

"My dear boy, that's all rubbish. The Secretary of War and I have minutely gone over the forces available for national defense. Mexico is a weak, backward country. It is poor. The morale of its inhabitants is low. It is impossible to conceive that it could successfully make war upon—" he paused, then rolled the words in his mouth—"upon the United States of America!" He turned to the Secretary of War, who sat cross-legged close to the desk.

The Secretary of War was a tall, thin man, whose hair rose in a bristly pompadour from a long, wrinkled face. He uncrossed his legs, recrossed them the other way, then said: "Of course, my dear young man! The whole idea is preposterous. We have given more freight to your hot-headed reports than we should—only because of your chief's insistence—" he nodded in the direction of the black-haired man who had admitted Operator 5—"of your chief's insistence that you have never been wrong in the past." He leaned forward in his chair, pointed a finger at Operator 5. "I have even gone so far as to concentrate the bulk of the Third Army in the Eighth Corps Area, along the Mexican Border—"

OPERATOR 5 interrupted him earnestly. "But don't you see, sir, that if my reports are well-founded, it is suicide for us to do that?"

He swung about, addressed all three men. "Let me go over the situation: A revolution has occurred in Mexico. A strange leader has arisen who calls himself Montezuma the Third, and who claims to be the rightful heir to the throne of the Aztec nation, which was overthrown by Cortez four hundred years ago. He has named himself Emperor of the Aztecs, and has set up temples to the ancient Aztec gods, where they sacrifice human beings by tearing out their hearts from their living bodies on the altars—"

The Secretary of War waved his hand in a gesture of impatience. "We know all that—"

The black-haired man who had admitted Operator 5 arose from behind his desk, his square, powerful fingers drumming a nervous tattoo on the glass top. He said: "Please, gentlemen! I suggest you wait until you hear everything that Operator 5 has to say."

This man behind the desk was known only by a number—Z-7. He was the Washington chief of the United States Intelligence Service. Through those blunt fingers of his passed the threads of every major intrigue that arose to menace the country; behind those raven-black eyes of his lurked more knowledge of matters vital to the country than even the Secretaries of State and of the Army could command. And they gave his unusual abilities a tremendous amount of grudging respect.

"Operator 5, gentlemen," he went on, "is the only man in the service whose judgment I respect without reservation. You could do worse," he added dryly, "than to hear him out!"

The Secretary of State shrugged, glanced at his fellow cabinet member, said: "Very well. Go on, Operator 5."

The young man turned eagerly to Z-7. "Chief! Let me have those reports in file 2318!"

Z-7 pressed a button at the side of his desk, and when a shirt-sleeved clerk appeared, ordered him to bring the file. In a moment Operator 5 was holding in his hand a thick sheaf of papers. He glanced keenly at both the cabinet members, riffled through the papers.

"Here, gentlemen, are a series of reports that have already been called to your attention. In Texas, in the last two days, there have been more than a dozen unaccountable deaths. Men have suddenly been killed—without warning—by exploding into bits! Among the victims are Major General Stanton, who was temporarily in command of the Third Army—"he read from the list—"Captain Polk, in charge of the Border Patrol; Captains Evans and Steele, and Lieutenant Worth of the flying corps, who were commanding Biggs, Hensley and Laredo Fields, respectively."

His keen eyes bored into them as he hammered home each point. "In New York, far away from the Mexican border, a Colonel Allison suddenly explodes into bits as he is entering the armory of the Twenty-third Field Artillery. There are other casualties—a list numbering fifty-one deaths. All these men *exploded*, gentlemen—exploded into bits of flesh and bone—*without any apparent cause!*"

His tone dropped, became confidential. "In the last two days, sirs, thirty-two airplanes took off from army bases, and did not return. We have every reason to believe that those planes haven't been destroyed—they have been forced to fly in a certain direction—"

HE WAS interrupted by a hurried tapping at the door. A clerk entered, with a typewritten message. "Sir!" the clerk blurted to Z-7. "T-this has just come in on the teletype from our San Antonio office!"

He handed the flimsy to Z-7 who glanced at it, paled, and looked up at the others. He nodded to the clerk, who turned and left. When the door had shut behind him, Z-7 said to them huskily: "Gentlemen, let me read this to you:

'... WDC-13... ENTIRE CONTINGENT BORDER PATROL WIPED OUT BY MYSTERIOUS EXPLOSION... HUNDRED AND FIFTY MEN BLOWN TO BITS... NO TRACE OF BOMB... CANNOT DISCOVER CAUSE... PLEASE RUSH US MORE MEN... SAT-1'"

He finished reading, glanced up at the two cabinet members. The Secretary of State snatched the flimsy from him, read it with his own eyes, then lifted his head and stared blankly at his colleague. The telephone on Z-7's desk jangled, interrupting him, and the Chief picked it up, answered it. Then he handed the instrument across to Operator 5.

He at once recognized the voice of the young Irish lad whom

he had left outside in the car. The boy's voice was tense with excitement.

"Jimmy! Vance Snyder is up to something. I spotted him coming out of the servants' entrance of Mrs. Hawkins' house, and I followed him. He walked down a couple of blocks, and went in a drugstore. By the time I got there, I just saw him come out of a phone booth, and I tailed him back to Mrs. Hawkins' house. He went in the same way!"

Operator 5 rapped out: "Okay, Tim. Get back to the car, and wait for me!"

He hung up, and his eyes bored into those of the Secretary of War. "Did you tell your nephew of this meeting, sir?" he demanded.

"Why—no. But I did tell him of this office. After all, he is my secretary."

"You should never have done that, sir!"

The Secretary of War flushed. "Young man!"

Jimmy Christopher was not listening. He had picked up the phone, and was jiggling the hook. "Give me Sommers... Sommers! Did Vance Snyder go out and return within the last few minutes? He did? He's on his way up? Have two men seize him and bring him to Z-7's office—at once! Yes, I know who he is. *Do what I say!*"

HE SLAMMED down the receiver, raised a hand to still the indignant protests of the Secretary of War. "Mr. Secretary, if your nephew is an innocent man I will be the first to apologize to him. But with things the way they are—"

He swung to the door as a knock sounded, pulled it open.

Vance Snyder stood there, panting in the grip of two of the Secret Service men.

Operator 5 ordered them quietly: "Let him come in, boys. You can go."

The two men were puzzled, but at a nod from Z-7 they obeyed.

Vance Snyder glanced at his uncle, rearranged his rumpled clothing. There was a hint of terror in his eyes as he blustered: "Who ordered that I be dragged up here? This is outrageous—"

Jimmy Christopher rapped out at him: "Snyder! Whom did you phone to a few minutes ago?"

The Secretary's nephew glared at Jimmy Christopher. "By what authority—?"

Jimmy's eyes were blazing. He stepped forward, seized Snyder by the lapels of his coat. "You fool! Tell me quickly! To whom did you phone and what did you tell that person?"

The Secretary of War arose from his chair. "See here, Operator 5! This has gone far enough. My nephew—"

Jimmy, still clutching Snyder's coat, whirled on the Secretary. "Your nephew," he said coldly, "just sneaked out of the servants' entrance of the house around the corner, and went to a public telephone booth to make a call."

The Secretary glanced at his nephew indulgently. "I am sure that Vance can explain everything." He addressed Snyder. "To satisfy Operator 5's baseless suspicions, Vance, tell him why you made that call."

Snyder lowered his eyes. "I don't see that it's any of his business," he said sulkily. "There's no law to prevent me from making a little extra money."

"What do you mean?" Jimmy Christopher demanded.

"Why—I have a newspaper friend who pays me for news tips. His paper is very generous. They're paying me five hundred dollars to tell them about this conference here. Of course, the paper won't state the location of this office—"

"So you told it to him in confidence?" Jimmy Christopher groaned.

Snyder fidgeted under Jimmy's powerful grip, nodded reluctantly. "Yes. But I assure you, it won't—"

Z-7 stepped quickly around the desk to interrupt. "What's the name of this newspaper friend? Who is he?"

Jimmy Christopher suddenly released his grip on Snyder's coat. He said swiftly to Z-7: "Wait, Chief. There's something more important than that right now. *You've got to empty this house of every man—at once!*"

Z-7 paled. "You mean—?"

"That Snyder here, has unwittingly been giving information to Montezuma and the Aztecs! He's not the only one. That's how they've been able to stage their explosions at crucial moments. I'm positive they're going to send their exploding death into this house! *They may be doing it now!*"

The Secretary of War deliberately sat down, stared at the others. His ruddy face was set stubbornly. "I won't leave here," he said. "I don't believe a word of this hair-brained operator of yours. I trust my nephew implicitly. You others may go if you

DOLORES

HORGAVO

are frightened—" his lip curled scornfully—"at what this scatterbrained young man tells you!"

Operator 5 met the gaze of Z-7. "And you, Chief?" he

MONTEZUMA THE THIRD

HELEN POWERS

asked. "Will you get all your men out of here before they're all destroyed?"

Z-7 looked at him helplessly. "I'm sorry, Operator 5," he murmured. "If the others stay—"

Operator 5 sighed. "Very well, gentlemen. I hope you don't mind if I go myself?"

He wheeled, strode for the door. Once out in the corridor, however, he did not make for the exit. Instead, he glanced quickly up and down to see if he was observed; then, with fingers that worked like oiled instruments of precision, he extracted from his pocket a small object made of aluminum.

It was a cone—no more than an inch and a half long and an inch in circumference at its base. He set it on the floor in a corner, lit a match and touched the flame to the apex. Almost at once, a thick mass of black smoke rose in the hallway, so dense that it was impossible to see anything through it. It spread rapidly, filling the hallway.

This was a device which Operator 5 had perfected in his own laboratory, and which he always carried with him in case it should become necessary for him to make a quick escape under cover of a smoke screen. The cone contained a skillfully blended mixture of phosphorus and chlorosulphoric acid—the chemical base of smoke screens ejected from the funnels of battleships. Although Operator 5 carried that cone for a different purpose, he found it useful now.

He felt his way through the dense cloud of smoke, jerked open the door of the room he had just left. The four men looked up in startled surprise as the thick clouds floated in.

Operator 5 shouted: "It's here! Get out quick!"

Z-7 jumped from behind his desk, seized the Secretary of War by the arm. "Come on, sir!" he exclaimed. "You can't doubt now!"

THE SECRETARIES of War and State, Vance Snyder and Z-7 rushed from the room, and Operator 5 followed them down the stairs. On the way, Z-7 issued swift orders to the men in the offices to evacuate the house, and a steady stream of shirt-sleeved workers hastened from the house, through the front door which had never been used before. Within a few minutes, the house was completely empty....

Out in the street, they gathered in small groups, watching the thick clouds of smoke that billowed from the building. Operator 5 stood close to Vance Snyder, with Z-7 and the two cabinet members. From afar they could hear the clangor of fire apparatus.

And suddenly, as they watched the house, there came a dull, muffled explosion from within it. Every pane of glass in the building was shattered; the shutters on the windows were thrust outward in splinters as by some invincible force. The air about them became thin, hard to breathe, and they backed further away.

The crashing, shattering noise of the explosion died away, leaving in the air the terrified cries of the crowding pedestrians who had stopped, astonished at the sudden exodus of men from a house they had believed to be empty.

The Secretary of War stared at his nephew, haggard-faced. "Vance!" he exclaimed.

Vance Snyder had been staring at the building with the eyes of a madman. Now he groaned: "God! What have I done?" And suddenly he thrust his uncle aside, sped across the street. In a moment he had reached the other side, and they saw him stagger,

saw blood spurt from his ears and nose. He stumbled forward another few steps, into the entrance....

And no sooner had he stepped within that house than he suddenly seemed to disintegrate! With a short, sharp explosion, he was torn into a thousand pieces. There was nothing left of the man who had been Vance Snyder....

Z-7 glanced somberly at Jimmy Christopher. "Now," he said, "We'll never know the name of his newspaper friend!"

The Secretary of War had covered his face with his hands. Now he raised his head, and his long, wrinkled face gray and drawn. He glanced wordlessly at the Secretary of State. Then he said to Jimmy Christopher: "Operator 5, everything you told us was correct. I don't know what to say, or what to do. We place ourselves in your hands!"

Jimmy nodded. He said crisply: "I suggest that you authorize me to fly to the Mexican border. If I'm right, the next move of the Aztecs will be to wipe our armed forces in Texas!"

CHAPTER 2
PRISONER OF THE AZTECS

T EXAS DUST swirled fitfully about the small group of temporary buildings comprising Provisional Headquarters of the Third Army, covering the Eighth Corps Area along the southern frontier of the United States.

Within the large, frame building which had only been completed an hour or so before dusk, a dozen executive officers sat at a long table. A gray-haired, haggard-featured man in uniform presided. His shoulder straps bore four silver stars—the insignia of a commanding general.

Outside, constant streams of infantry and artillery plodded by, the enlisted men—entirely unaware that they were marching to almost certain death. The officers at that table in Provisional Headquarters, however, knew it only too well....

They talked in low, grim tones. There was a strange expression in the eyes of all of them—the look of brave men who know Death waits for them, yet who cannot understand its nature. Most men are willing to fight for a righteous cause against a known force. But it takes brave men indeed to face death in a horrible, unknown manner....

The man at the head of the table was addressing the others: "Gentlemen," he said in weary tones, "I have just had a report from the front. The Aztecs are advancing across the border. Major-General Oppington reports that he has lost five hundred troops without being able to strike a blow. The artillery cannot be brought into action—each gun crew that approaches a piece

31

of ordnance immediately explodes into bits—as if by a time bomb. Our planes go up, and then seem to set a direct course for Mexico. Not one of them returns. Whole squads of men defending our positions are suddenly exploded, and the Aztecs march ahead without opposition. Gentlemen—" The general arose at the head of the table. His eyes lowered before the gaze of the assembled officers. "I have ordered Major-General Oppington to fall back!"

A stocky, bullet-headed colonel of Intelligence leaped to his feet at the opposite end of the table. "Do you mean to say, sir, that you ordered a retreat? We have thirty thousand men in this corps area; are we to run away from a rabble of peons and mestizos led by a madman who has named himself an emperor?"

The general sighed wearily. "Why not, Colonel? We are faced by some mysterious force that we cannot understand. Our men explode from within—as if they had swallowed dynamite. Do you expect me to send more of our boys out to be slaughtered in the same way? God, man—" the general's face was twisted with passion—"it—it's uncanny, gruesome; like marching against eternity. I won't do it, I tell you! I won't sacrifice any more lives!"

"But, sir," the colony protested, "if Major-General Oppington retreats, it will leave no opposition between the Aztecs and Fort Sam Houston. If the Aztecs take Houston, they'll have a solid footing in the United States!"

The general shrugged. "Let them take it, Colonel Lacon. I'll order Houston evacuated. The Aztecs will have to hold up their advance there for at least a day in order to organize their position and bring up provisions. It'll give us a breathing spell—"

He stopped as a second lieutenant entered, saluted and said: "Colonel Grant's respects, sir. The Fifty-sixth Regiment is ready to be reviewed, sir, before marching."

The general nodded and the lieutenant left. The staff officers all gazed at their commander gravely. He turned from the table said slowly: "I'll review them, anyway. But I'm going to countermand their marching orders."

The officers followed him out into the night. Flares lighted the entire field. Regimental bands were playing as men marched by. A whole regiment of United States infantry—a powerful, almost invincible fighting machine, stepping as one man; fifteen hundred men, comprising a unit of military strength that could have routed a dozen Roman legions.

The general sighed as he and his staff saluted the passing colors. "I wish," he murmured to his aide, "that the man they're sending from Washington would come soon. It'll be a relief to turn over the responsibility for all these men to someone else." He gulped, as his aide eyed him sympathetically. "God! I have never shirked responsibility before in my life. But this—"

HIS WORDS were drowned by the sudden thunderous explosion that seemed to roll over the field of marching men. Suddenly all those uniformed men seemed to disintegrate before the very eyes of the general and his staff. Individual explosions followed each other with crackling rapidity as if an immense hand were sweeping over the field and touching a match to groups of firecrackers, one after the other.

Bits of flesh and bone, bits of torn clothing, filled the air, rained down upon the heads of the transfixed staff. The air grew stifling, hard to breathe, filled with the stench of scorched flesh. A haze gathered over the field through which it was difficult to see.

And abruptly as it had come, the holocaust passed. The air cleared slightly. And the general and his staff stared with dread-filled eyes at that field. Not a single man of that marching regiment was left alive. The ground was strewn with blood and bits of flesh and torn clothing. In the space of one minute an entire regiment had been annihilated as by a breath from some unseen god!

The general staggered backward, leaned against the wall of his headquarters for support. Suddenly he had become an old man. He tried to speak, but no words came from his lips. He could only gaze in stupefaction at his officers.

And from far above to the north, there came to their ears the drone of a plane. The colonel of Intelligence gulped, said: "T-that must be the man from Washington, sir. My God! He's come just in time to see death and destruction!"

The general pulled himself together. "This is the end!" he grated hoarsely. "We can't fight a thing like this. When that plane lands, I'm going to turn over—"

"Wait, sir!" the colonel of Intelligence exclaimed. "His motor's cut out. He's coming from the north, with the wind. He couldn't be landing that way. He's out of control!"

Indeed, the heavy army transport seemed to be acting erratically above that field of carnage. It swooped low over the heads of the staff officers, with the motor dead; then once more they heard it cough, burst into its droning roar. It was working again.

They watched the pilot climb, try to bank, and once more they strained eagerly as they heard the engine go dead.

Again and again, white stretcher bearers patrolled the field in a vain search for a single living man, the general and his aides watched that plane try to veer into the wind for a landing; and each time they heard the engine die.

The colonel of Intelligence exclaimed: "He can't make it, sir. His motor is all right, but there's some sort of air pocket up there that cuts it off. What?"

He ceased talking, watched intently as a small figure legged over the side of the plane, hurtled toward them. A parachute billowed out, the sudden drop of the figure was broken, and they all ran toward the spot where he would fall.

Before they got there, the figure landed. Several enlisted men helped him out of his parachute harness, and he stood erect just as General Everard and his staff came running up.

The general came to a halt, staring in amazement, as did the other officers, at the freckle-faced, tough-looking Irish lad who faced them.

General Everard demanded: "Who in tarnation are you? How did you get into that army plane?"

But the boy paid him no attention for the moment. He was gazing upward anxiously, watching the transport. It was now a good distance away, winging its way southward. His lips moved, and he said under his breath, with his eyes still on the plane: "Good luck to you, Jimmy! I wish—" his lips trembled, and he gulped a little—"that you'd let me go along!"

Abruptly the boy turned, drew from his pocket a slip of paper.

"General Everard?" he asked, eyeing the four silver stars on that officer's uniform. The general nodded, puzzlement and irritation showing in his seamed face. "This message is for you, general, from Operator 5—the man you were expecting from Washington. He wrote it up there in the plane when he found we couldn't land."

THE GENERAL took the slip of paper, growled: "I don't understand this. Instead of a man they send me a boy—!" His words trailed off as he read the note by the glare of one of the flares:

> To General Everard, Commanding Third Army:
> Impossible to land due to mysterious atmospheric conditions. We are being compelled, by some strong power, to fly south toward the area under occupation by the Aztecs. Our radio sending-set does not function. Apparently the Aztecs plan to force us to land within their lines and to capture us. I shall do so in hope of securing valuable information. In the meantime, would advise you retreat upon Fort Sam Houston. The bearer of this note is Tim Donovan, my unofficial assistant. Keep him close to you, as any messages I may be able to send will be in code which he can easily read.
>
> Operator 5.

General Everard glanced up from the strange note, written hastily in pencil, eyed the boy. "How do I know," he demanded, "that this is authentic? How do I know that the man who wrote this note is really Operator 5? How do I know that your name is—" he looked at the paper—"Tim Donovan?"

Tim Donovan said quietly: "That is easily proved, sir." He glanced at the colonel of Intelligence, raised his right hand. Upon his finger there gleamed a ring with a death's-head skull, peculiarly fashioned. "You are an Intelligence officer, sir," he said. "Do you recognize this ring?"

The colonel took the boy's hand in his own, studied the ring. Then he nodded. "This is the ring, General Everard. All Intelligence officers have been instructed. There is a certain mark on it that identifies it as authentic. This boy is really Tim Donovan, who has been assisting Operator 5 remarkably well for some time. This lad is too young to be admitted to the Secret Service yet, but—"

Tim Donovan said urgently: "If you're satisfied about me, general, let's get to a wireless receiving-set as quickly as possible. Ji—I mean—Operator 5, may send through a message at any moment."

The general nodded. "All right. Operator 5 is our only hope now. The Aztecs seem to be able to annihilate our entire forces at will. Guns are no good against them!"

IN THE army plane, which was soon lost to sight in the engulfing darkness to the south of provisional headquarters, the pilot sat grim-lipped at his controls. Behind him, his passenger stared ahead through the night. Jimmy Christopher, known in the Secret Service only as Operator 5, had taken off his own helmet and goggles, and was gazing ahead, regardless of the furious wind that lashed at him. His sharp, intelligent, clean-cut face was like that of some young god, riding the skies fearlessly toward whatever fate might hold....

Down below he could see, faintly in the night, the terrain of Texas—broad, parched fields upon which there was no life whatsoever. But soon the panorama changed. Little, motionless dots flecked the landscape below—thousands of them. Jimmy Christopher's pulse raced. He knew only too well what those little dots were—the pitiable, torn remains of what had once been stalwart United States Army soldiers, and their officers; all horridly mangled and torn by this strange force that Montezuma controlled.

Far to the east were dark moving specks—the remnants of the first line divisions in retreat. And soon there came into the range of Operator 5's vision the forces of the Aztecs, encamped in a huge circle upon the plain.

He tapped the pilot on the shoulder, motioned to him to attempt a landing. The pilot nodded, and the plane veered down. And almost at once the twin motors sputtered, grew silent!

Jimmy Christopher felt a strange tightness in the atmosphere; breathing became more difficult. Frantically the pilot fought his controls, managed to keep the plane level. And in a moment, the motors coughed, resumed their rhythmic beat. The plane spurted ahead, and the pilot turned his head to Jimmy, his lips formed panicky words: "They won't let us land! We've got to go on!"

Operator 5 nodded. His face was eager with expectation. He motioned the pilot to continue along the same course. They had enough fuel to keep them in the air for hours. There was no immediate danger.

Below them there passed in swift panorama the huge encampment of the Aztec invaders—thousands upon thousands of orderly tents, with watch fires burning brightly. Those invaders, he reflected bitterly, were safe from attack by the troops of the United States. Every detachment that had advanced against them had been destroyed by the invisible force—the same invisible power that was compelling this plane to continue on its southward course.

They passed a thin, twisting silver band that bisected the earth below; Jimmy Christopher knew it was the Rio Grande. Now they were over Mexico....

Several times the pilot tried to descend, and each time the same phenomenon occurred—the motors went dead until he brought the plane up again, in the path of its southward flight. It was uncanny, chilling; the feeling that unseen eyes were watching them, driving them along.

At last, Jimmy's sharp eyes discerned the gleaming sheen of water. He drew in his breath sharply at the beauty of the scene below him—Mexico City, sitting high on its natural plateau, on the edge of Lake Tezcuco.

The white macadam roads leading toward the city were covered with moving lines of men and trucks, marching northward. More forces for the invasion of America! And far over the plateau were more moving masses of men; a mere handful against the vast armies which the United States could muster, but invincible now with the aid of the terrible weapon that their master had acquired....

And now, when the pilot attempted to veer into the wind and land, there was no dying of motors. The plane dropped slowly under his skillful manipulation toward a field to the east of the city, illuminated by huge incandescent bulbs....

A LINE of Aztec infantry was drawn up to meet them as the plane coasted to a stop, and mechanics ran out to help them.

When the motors were shut off, Jimmy Christopher said to the pilot: "Here we are, lieutenant. Keep a stiff upper lip. They didn't bring us here just to sacrifice us on their alters. But if we have to die, let's go out like men!"

They shook hands, descended from the plane. A tall man in brilliant uniform stepped forward, saluted gravely. He was lean-featured, thin-lipped, with sharp eyes that roved over Jimmy's well-knit figure like those of a hangman. There was a note of wonder in his voice as he said: "Are you then, that so dangerous person who is known as Operator 5? I expected an older man."

Jimmy said curtly: "I am Operator 5."

"That, my friend," the officer said, "is but a number. What is your name?"

Jimmy grinned. "Operator 5 will have to do you. Only my friends call me by name."

The officer smiled thinly. "You are another of those who need coaxing, no? No matter. At the palace we will know how to make you loquacious. Come!"

He turned, stalked across the landing field. A file of soldiers opened, took position on either side of Jimmy. Jimmy said to the pilot: "They don't want you, old man. Stay by the plane if you can."

The two men shook hands, and the pilot said earnestly: "Good luck, Operator 5!"

At the edge of the field, a large closed car was waiting. The Aztec officer got in first, then Jimmy was motioned in. Two soldiers sat on the rear seat, on either side of him, while the officer sat on one of the forward folding seats. The car got in motion.

Jimmy said: "Would it be too much, sir, to ask where we are going?"

The officer turned his head, gazed at him a moment, then answered: "You are being taken to an interview with our emperor—Montezuma the Third. Be careful how you speak to him. If you are wise, you will answer his questions more fully than you have answered mine."

Jimmy relaxed in his seat, thoughtfully. Why Montezuma should have gone to this trouble to bring him here, he could guess. As Operator 5 of the United States Secret Service, it might well be assumed that he was in possession of all the secrets of defense of the country. If they should torture him....

Jimmy Christopher's lips set firmly.

CHAPTER 3
THE PRINCESS DOLORES

L OOKING THROUGH the windows of the swiftly moving car, Jimmy Christopher could see the feverish military activity on all sides. This small country of sixteen million people had overnight become a warrior nation. Only a few months ago there had come out of the province of Zacatecas a man who claimed to be of pure Aztec blood—a direct descendant of the haughty, cruel Montezuma who had been emperor of the Aztecs when the Spaniards conquered Mexico. He called himself Montezuma the Third. Indians and mestizos flocked to him. The Mexican government had viewed this at first as only another chronic rising, to be quelled quickly.

But the authorities soon learned their mistake. Montezuma was possessed of a mysterious force which destroyed the detachments of Nationalist soldiers sent against him. In a short time, he was master of Mexico, had proclaimed himself Emperor. And now he was extending his conquest to the United States! If Operator 5 did not quickly discover the secret of this strange power which Montezuma wielded, his country would soon be a vassal of the Aztec Empire!

Jimmy Christopher continued to watch the progress of the car, saw they were racing along a wide, concrete causeway toward a huge castle-like structure about a half-mile away. The causeway stretched like a long, white ribbon straight ahead of them, over a glittering body of water upon the edge of which the palace was built.

To the right and left of them were other causeways. These roads were crowded with Aztec soldiers marching in slovenly fashion. Jimmy glanced sideways at the brilliantly uniformed, thin-lipped officer who sat next to him, saw that the man  was watching him through sharp, narrowed eyes. "Do you speak Spanish?" he asked, and when Jimmy nodded, he immediately changed to that language. "Permit me to introduce myself. I am Major Juan Horgavo, the head of the Aztec Intelligence Bureau. I have heard many tales of you, Operator 5, and I am surprised to find that you are so young."

Jimmy answered dryly: "Thanks for the compliment. How did you know I was in that plane?"

Horgavo raised his eyebrows. "We know nearly everything that goes on in Washington, Operator 5. Our agents are everywhere."

Jimmy Christopher grinned. "Pretty good organizer, aren't you, major? When the Aztecs are licked, and you're looking for another job, let me know and I'll give you a reference."

The major's teeth showed in a wolfish smile. "You Americans are so rash in your talk. You are all fools. You will change your tune when our torturers have worked on you for a while. You—"

He stopped as the car swung off the causeway into a wide drive, braking under an immense portico.

A squad of soldiers under a junior officer were drawn up to receive them, and Major Horgavo got out first, then bowed ironically, murmured: "Welcome to Mexico City, Operator 5!"

Jimmy grimaced, and descended from the car. At a sharp command from Horgavo, the squad of soldiers divided, took positions on either side. They marched through the aisle of men to the broad entrance and into the huge palace.

Here there was much scurrying and bustle. Men in uniform were everywhere. All saluted Horgavo with great respect and cast curious eyes on the prisoner. Jimmy, with his military escort, ascended a broad flight of stairs, marched along another hall, and finally stopped before a huge, oak door.

Major Horgavo motioned to the junior officer, who produced a pair of handcuffs. The Aztec intelligence commander murmured to Jimmy: "I hope you will not object. No prisoner is permitted to appear in the presence of the emperor unbound."

Jimmy shrugged, extended his hands. The officer slipped the handcuffs on him, then quickly searched Jimmy, took the automatic from his shoulder holster, as well as a thin, flat silver case. He handed the case to Horgavo, who, still smiling with mock courtesy, opened it. Within the case was revealed a typed sheet of paper which read:

THE WHITE HOUSE
Washington

To Whom It May Concern:

The identity of the bearer of this letter must be kept strictly confidential.

He is Operator 5 of the United States Intelligence Service.

The signature at the bottom of the document was that of the President of the United States of America.

HORGAVO NODDED in satisfaction. "This is what I wanted to make sure of," he said. "You are the man whom our emperor wishes to see!"

He turned, and at a word from him, the guard opened the big oak door. They passed into a huge room at the far end of which was a raised dais. Men in brilliant uniform filled this room, but the figure on the dais outshone them all. Montezuma the Third sat there upon a chair of gold, clad in a gold-embroidered mantle which must have cost a fortune. Upon his head rested a glittering crown, and at his side, in a scabbard, hung a short sword whose hilt was cunningly fashioned into the head of a bird of prey.

The emperor's face was long and thin, with a sharp, straight nose and a cruel gash of a mouth almost hidden by his mustache and carefully trimmed beard. The haughty, predatory features reminded Jimmy Christopher of pictures he had seen of the earlier Montezuma. He reflected that it was quite possible for this man to be a direct descendant of the Emperor of the Aztecs.

Jimmy was propelled across the room by his guards, and he approached the dais. Horgavo bowed low before the emperor, bending himself almost double, and said reverentially: "Lord, my Lord, my great Lord!"

Montezuma raised his hand to the others in the room,

Jimmy raised the rifle, drew
a bead on the Emperor!

ordered imperiously: "Leave us!" There were some forty or fifty
men there, and they all backed meekly out the doorway.

When they were alone, Horgavo said humbly: "Master, I
bring you Operator 5. By projection, we forced his plane to fly
directly here."

Montezuma's black, piercing eyes settled on Jimmy. He spoke in English with only a slight accent. "Operator 5, do you know why I had you brought to me?"

Jimmy shook his head. He was studying the other, trying to decide what manner of man this was who had made himself Emperor of the Aztecs—overnight.

"For five days, Operator 5, I have caused my priests to make sacrifice upon the altars of the old gods of the Aztecs—Huitzilopochtli and Tezcatlipoca. In the old tradition of our beliefs, we offered the still palpitating hearts of hundreds of your captured countrymen upon the altars, asking our gods to give us an omen that would bring us victory. And our gods spoke. They told us to find a certain man who was known as Operator 5."

Jimmy, returning the stare of Montezuma, said dryly:

"Are you sure it was your gods that spoke, or was it the tortured lips of some of my countrymen?"

Montezuma smiled. "You are bold, Operator 5. I like bold men. I like to see them writhe before they die. After you have served your—"

Suddenly, from somewhere behind the curtains which hung in back of the dais, came a shriek of agony. It filled the whole room, seeming to have been torn from a tortured throat by red-hot, demoniac fingers.

Operator 5's flashing blue eyes became cloudy and dark. His lips pressed into a thin line, and his manacled hands clenched in front of him. He took an involuntary step toward the dais, but was roughly seized by his guards, held back.

He said tightly: "I give you my word, Montezuma, that my

country will exact terrible vengeance for every one of its men whom you torture!"

Montezuma's face became ugly with rage for an instant, and he half rose from his throne. Then he smiled thinly, said softly: "Your country, Operator 5, will bow its head in abject submission!"

"Never!" Jimmy said hoarsely. "The United States will never surrender to a barbarian race led by a madman like you!"

Montezuma's face darkened. He grated: "You are too bold." He stopped, for once more that shriek sounded from behind the dais, chilling Jimmy Christopher's soul, then it died away in a soft gurgle of agony. From behind the curtains came the roll of a drum in a dreadful, funereal cadence. Then the sound of many jabbering voices.

JIMMY CHRISTOPHER watched, white-faced, while Montezuma rang a bell at his elbow. Immediately, the curtains behind the dais parted, and a tall Aztec, clad in a long, white robe that was spattered with blood, entered, bowed low. This man had a gaunt face with deep-set eyes under heavy, bushy brows. His teeth were big, and glistened as he spoke in a tongue that Jimmy could not understand, but which he guessed to be the language of the ancient Aztec nation.

Montezuma listened carefully, until the man had ceased talking. Then he smiled in satisfaction, said to Jimmy:

"My high priest brings me most interesting information. He has just made another sacrifice to Tezcatlipoca, our god of war; and Tezcatlipoca has spoken, telling us your true name. You are

James Christopher. Your father, John Christopher, was once known as Q-6 in the American Intelligence Service. Is it not so?"

Jimmy Christopher's face flushed. "No god told you that, Montezuma! That devilish priest of yours has just tortured some poor captive into revealing who I am. Who was that man who just shrieked?"

Montezuma smiled thinly, motioned to the high priest, said something to him in their own tongue. The high priest bowed, stepped back to draw the curtains aside. "I will show you, Operator 5," Montezuma said softly. "So that you may know what fate to expect yourself!" The priest drew back the curtains, and at a sign from Montezuma, Jimmy's guards urged him around the dais so that he could see what lay behind it.

There was a small room there, windowless, except for a large opening cut into the stone of the roof. In one corner sat a large, ugly idol, fat, revolting. This was the god, Tezcatlipoca, half man and half serpent. It was carved out of stone, about five times the size of a normal man, and about its fat throat hung a necklace of human skulls. Some of them were fresh—still dripping blood.

On the floor before the gruesome idol lay a man, stripped to the waist, and stretched upon a wooden rack to which his hands and feet had been nailed. Jimmy gazed down with wide eyes at the agonized, pain-distorted face of the man. This was one whom he knew well—F-13, one of the most trusted agents of the Secret Service. F-13 was one of the few men who knew Operator 5's true identity. He had been sent down into Mexico only a few days before, in company with Jimmy's own father, who, in spite of a bad heart, had insisted upon serving his country in this grave, new peril.

Now he saw F-13 lying nailed to that rack, dying. And he saw the long bloody furrows on F13's body, where Montezuma's torturers had torn strips of skin from his living body to make him talk. F-13's torso was a bloody thing of pain and agony, and Jimmy Christopher's face was gray and drawn as he knelt, handcuffed, beside the dying Secret Service man.

"F-13!" he said in a choked voice. "I promise you they'll pay for this!"

F-13 stared up at him through filming eyes. He said huskily: "I—I couldn't stand the torture. They—they made me talk, made me tell your name. I—God! I'm a skunk. I should have kept quiet. Now they know—"

Jimmy Christopher forced a smile. "Don't worry, old man. No harm will come to me. You should have talked—sooner!"

F-13's face twisted into a pain-wracked smile. "Thanks, Operator 5. I—I know—you're trying to make me feel—better. I shouldn't—have—talked!" Suddenly, a spasm of pain shot through his body. A low moan tore through his tortured lips. His eyes glazed, and his body stiffened. He was dead.

Jimmy Christopher arose slowly from his knees. He whispered: "God forgive you, F-13, and save your soul!"

His darkening eyes sought those of Montezuma, who had stood in the doorway watching the scene. The two guards felt Jimmy's body stiffening as if for a leap, and their hard hands clamped on his arms. But Jimmy did not move. He recognized the foolhardiness of attempting to spring upon the bloody emperor. For beside Montezuma stood Horgavo, a loaded automatic in his hand. Jimmy would only have thrown away his life fruitlessly.

MONTEZUMA WAS smiling maddeningly. "There are certain things we wish to know from you, Operator 5. Even if you do not care what happens to you, you will not wish to see your father in the hands of our priests. Come, I will show you more. Perhaps then you will be more ready to answer Major Horgavo's questions!" He turned, led the way out. Jimmy cast a last glance back at the dead, distorted body of F-13, and followed, propelled by his guards. Horgavo stood in the doorway, smiling ironically.

Jimmy asked him: "Where is my father?"

"Your father," Horgavo replied, "has not been harmed—yet." And he stepped back so that Jimmy and his guards could pass through.

Outside, in the corridor, the guards bowed reverently as Montezuma passed them. They crossed a courtyard, entered another wing of the palace. Jimmy Christopher, still in the grip of his captors, still manacled, followed Montezuma silently.

At length they arrived at another room, where a dozen officers were assembled. There was another raised dais in this room, and Montezuma mounted it while all the officers bowed reverently, saying: "Lord, my Lord, my great Lord!" As they said it, they bowed almost to the floor.

Jimmy gazed at them scornfully for a moment, and then his eyes settled on the fiery-eyed, darkly beautiful woman who stood beside the dais. She did not bow like the others, but held her head high, proudly, haughtily. Her figure was encased in some sort of clinging, red-silk gown that trailed on the floor, and her black hair was done up into a great knot at the back off her neck.

Jimmy noted at once the resemblance she bore to the emperor. He was not surprised when Montezuma, after seating himself, said to her: "My daughter, this is the man of whom you have heard—Operator 5 of the United States Secret Service. You remember that our agents informed us about him, but regretted that he was too clever to capture?"

The girl's cruel, red mouth curved in a slow smile as she inspected Jimmy Christopher. Her dark flashing eyes studied him with a sort of feline interest as she breathed: "Yes, I have heard much about him. I am very glad he is our prisoner."

Jimmy Christopher shuddered inwardly as she spoke. There was revealed in her eyes a cruelty fully equal to that of her father. And there was something else—something that he had seen in the eyes of many women, but hoped to find only in the eyes of one. For Operator 5 was good to look at. He was clean-cut, blue-eyed, with the broad shoulders and narrow hips of an athlete. And despite his youth, he was possessed of a poise that many an older man might have envied; for his life had been packed with danger and action and strange experiences—which are the doings that fashion a man out of a youth.

Now the girl said softly, with the air of one who is accustomed to getting anything that she wants: "Do not kill him, father—yet. I would like—to know him better!"

Montezuma chuckled. "You shall have him, Dolores, as soon as I am through with him." He suddenly became brusque. "But now—let us get to business. We are here to pass judgment upon a culprit. Bring him in!"

At a sign from one of the officers at the door, two guards led in a trembling Aztec soldier, who seemed to shrink away from the august presence of the emperor as he was dragged toward the dais.

He was perhaps forty-five years old, well built. But his face was pale and drawn with pain. Jimmy Christopher saw that he had been tortured—the fingers of both his hands hung at queer angles; all had been broken!

When the man stood before the dais, half supported by the two guards, Montezuma said: "What is this man accused of, and who is the complainant?"

THE BEAUTIFUL Dolores took a single step forward. "I am the complainant, father. This man failed to salute me when I passed him this morning. For that, the fingers of his hands have been crushed between two rocks. But I demand further punishment."

The man with the broken fingers raised both his hands in supplication. Sweat beaded his forehead, and his hands, with their gruesome broken fingers, trembled. "Great Lord!" he cried. "Do not torture me further—!"

Montezuma frowned at him, and the man subsided into frightened silence. "What punishment do you wish for him, Dolores!" the emperor asked.

Dolores said coldly: "Let him die," and tossed her head in contempt.

Montezuma nodded. "It is right. We must set an example for

the other soldiers. My daughter's person is as sacred as my own. Those who forget their respect toward us must die."

The poor wretch with the broken fingers screamed: "Mercy, my lord. Mercy! Mercy!"

But at a look from Montezuma, Horgavo, who had been standing on the other side of the dais from Dolores, motioned to the guards, and they dragged the man, struggling, screaming for mercy, to a wide French window that faced on the courtyard. The window was open, and they thrust him out, sent him sprawling to the flagstones.

The man struggled to his feet, raising himself up on his wrists to avoid resting on his broken fingers. He turned a piteous, pleading face toward them; but Horgavo, who had come close to the window, raised his arm in some sort of signal. And suddenly, with horrid abruptness, the man outside seemed to explode *from within!*

His body seemed to have been torn to a thousand bits, as if there had been a time-bomb within him. Blood spattered the flagstones, bits of flesh and bone hurtled through the air. And in a moment all was quiet again. The big incandescents in the courtyard threw a glittering light on the bloody pavement.

And through the sudden stillness that followed, rang the brittle laughter of the woman Dolores. She was *laughing!* Laughing at the sight of a man blasted into bloody shreds because he had failed to salute her. And Operator 5 realized she was beautiful—beautiful even in her cold, heartless amusement. Her eyes were flashing with the sadistic pleasure of some medieval princess, and her laughter echoed in the large, stone room, while Horgavo bowed in her direction with a smirk on his face.

And it was at that moment, when the attention of everyone in the room was focused on the bloody event that had just taken place, that Jimmy Christopher acted—with the swift sureness that had made him the ace of the United States Intelligence.

The grip of his two guards was still tight on his arms, but their eyes were on the courtyard. Jimmy twisted his body to the left, then lunged right, allowing his weight to break the grip of the guards. For a fraction of a second, he was free; and in that instant of time, he raised his manacled hands, brought them down hard on the skull of the guard at his right. The man dropped like a plummet. Jimmy dropped with him, picking up the rifle that the unconscious soldier had dropped!

The second guard, with a vicious expression on his face, had raised his own clubbed gun. In a moment, he would have brained Operator 5 with it; but Jimmy, from his position on the floor, shot out both his legs to catch the guard in a powerful scissors hold that sent him toppling off balance.

Then, as the second guard crashed to the floor, Jimmy Christopher rolled over, uncoiled his legs and catapulted toward the doorway, holding in his manacled hands the rifle he had picked up.

The superbly swift reaction of his trained muscles brought him to the door before any one of the assembled officers could raise a finger to stop him. There, Jimmy, with a face grim as granite, turned, raised the rifle awkwardly to his shoulder and drew a bead on the august figure of Montezuma....

Even in that split second when he leaped for the door, he had realized that this was the only thing to do. With Montezuma dead, the whole attack against the United States would collapse, leaderless. Jimmy himself might be torn to pieces by the enraged followers of the emperor, but his own life was a small price to pay for the safety of America.

Jimmy's finger curled around the trigger while the brilliantly uniformed officers stood rooted to the floor. Only one person in that whole room thought quickly—Montezuma's daughter, Dolores. With the grace of a tigress she stepped in front of her father, facing Jimmy's rifle.

There was a tenseness in her eyes, and her whole body was quivering under its red sheath of a dress.

JIMMY'S EYES clouded. In spite of the heartless cruelty which she had just shown, he could not bring himself to send a slug of lead crashing into that beautiful breast. Into his mind there flashed the words that Z-7, his chief, had often spoken: "In the Secret Service, we cease to become human beings—we become numbers. We must have no emotions, no mercy, no loves; we must be machines. And we must destroy whatever threatens our country!"

Jimmy tightened his lips. This woman was beautiful, cruel—but she was brave. He steeled himself to shoot—and it was too late!

Dolores' action had pricked the panicky lethargy of the officers. With shouts of rage, they hurled themselves at Jimmy, forming a well of living flesh between his rifle and the body of their emperor. Guns appeared in their hands. One exploded, crashing in the confines of the room; but Jimmy had already ducked around the edge of the doorway, out into the corridor.

He collided with the guard stationed outside the doorway, whirled, and brought the muzzle of the rifle up sharply against the guard's chin. The uniformed man staggered backward, reeled against the wall, sank to the floor....

Jimmy, gripping the rifle in his manacled hands, dashed, zigzagging, down the corridor, turned a corner just as a hail of lead thundered after him from the weapons of the officers who had stormed out of the room. He sped down the bend of the corridor. A broad flight of stone stairs loomed before him, and he knew he could not get to the top of it before his pursuers reached the bend. They would be able to pick him off with ease as he ran up. So he raced past the foot of the stairs, swung in behind the staircase. There was an open door here, and a flight of steps led down into darkness. Jimmy did not hesitate. He stepped through the doorway, reached out and swung the door shut behind him. In the dark, he felt his way down the narrow steps with one hand against the wall.

The steps seemed unending. The air grew foul and dank, the wall slimy and wet under his touch. He reached a landing, stepped cautiously until he found more steps, and continued his descent.

At last, the staircase ended in some sort of platform, and Operator 5 risked putting on his flashlight. He found that he had come down into a narrow, vaulted passageway that seemed to lead around the palace. The sound of a low, chanting voice came to him from somewhere at the left.

He made his way toward that sound, clicking off his light, and feeling along the side wall. The old Aztec palaces, he recalled reading, had been honeycombed with secret passages, with underground dungeons, and with torture chambers. There was an old story to the effect that one of the temples of the god, Huitzilopochtli, was located underneath the earth in the palace of Montezuma, and that it had been the scene of rites too obscene to be exposed to the light of day. It was in this underground temple that the Aztecs had secretly sacrificed living beings after the Spanish conquerors under Cortez had forbidden the practice.

It was entirely possible that he was now in one of the passages of the old temple. He worked swiftly along now, turned a bend in the passageway, and glimpsed, at a little distance away, a dull shaft of light which was coming across the stone flags from somewhere. The sound of the chanting gained in volume.

Jimmy headed for the light, found that it came from a low, wide-grilled opening on the right. He crept up close, and the chanting ceased. He risked peering through the opening, and he crouched there, frozen with horror.

This must indeed be the secret underground sacrificial temple of which legend had spoken.

The grilled opening was close to the ceiling of the room into which he looked....

CHAPTER 4
CHAMBER OF SACRIFICE

THE ROOM beneath Operator 5 was immense, lighted by tapers that stood in sconces along the walls. At the far end, directly opposite the window, was a great stone image of a repulsive god—Huitzilopochtli, half serpent and half man. Before the god was a stone altar, smeared with dried blood.

Two bearded priests, with close-shaven heads, in white robes, stood on the altar. A man was staked out on his back, at their feet, tied to a rack similar to the one upon which F-13 had died. This man was dead also, and Jimmy's blood grew hot with revulsion as he realized the manner of the victim's death. He had been offered as a sacrifice in the ancient Aztec manner; the heart had been torn from his body, and one of the priests was even now holding the gory thing in his hands, offering it before the ghastly idol.

The dead man was stripped to the waist, and his torso was bathed in his own blood. Jimmy saw the lower part of the man's body was clothed in puttees of olive drab. He had been an officer of the United States Army—probably captured in the first advance of the Aztecs when they had overrun southeastern Texas.

Along both side walls of this room there were small iron cages, about two dozen in all. And in each of these cages was a man, sitting in a crouching position, because there was not enough room to straighten. These were the sacrificial victims who would follow the one now on the altar. The Aztecs always

fattened those whom they prepared for the sacrifice—Huitzilopochtli did not like lean and scrawny offerings.

The two priests now prostrated themselves before the stone
god, and Jimmy's eyes roved from one cage to another—seeking
a certain face. He dreaded to see the features of his father in one
of those cages. But he did.

In the third cage from the altar John Christopher was
crouched in the narrow cubicle, head bowed in prayer.

Jimmy's lips tightened. He took from the lining of his coat a
thin, tempered steel saw sheathed in a small chamois scabbard.
He removed the scabbard with his teeth, proceeded to file at
one of the bars. But at the first rasp of the saw, one of the priests
rose, gazed toward the window suspiciously. Jimmy drew back.
He was in darkness, of course, but he did not know how sharp
the eyes of the white-robed votary of Huitzilopochtli might be.

The second priest got to his knees, and the two of them whispered together for a moment. Then one of them shrugged, and
they returned to their devotions. Jimmy surmised that they
considered it impossible for an enemy to have reached that
window.

They prostrated themselves once more, and Jimmy knew
they would remain there for hours, hoping that their god would
vouchsafe them some word of advice or prophecy in return for
the sacrifice.

He dared not resume his sawing, lest he attract their attention again.

Suddenly Jimmy noticed that his father had turned his head
and was gazing through red-rimmed eyes up at the grilled

Operator 5's automatic sprang into his
hand like a live thing and barked twice...!

window. The other prisoners in the cages were lethargic, hopeless, not even casting a glance at the grisly figure of their dead compatriot on the altar. But John Christopher, in spite of the obvious torture of his cramped position, in spite of the awful fate that seemed to be in store for him, was alert and keen.

Jimmy's pulse raced as he saw his father's face, gray and lined, with a four or five day growth of beard, looking up in his direction.

HE WAITED, breathless, watching his father. And then a slow, glad smile spread over Jimmy's face. For John Christopher had begun to sing!

In his deep baritone voice that Jimmy remembered listening to so fervently in his childhood days, John Christopher began to chant the august, cadenced measures of "The Battle Hymn of the Republic!"

The priests looked up, disturbed, from their prostrate devotions; then shrugged, and returned to their prayers. No doubt they thought that the prisoner was seeking surcease in song. And slowly the other prisoners, cheered by the slow swing of the majestic melody, joined in, until the room was filled with sound.

Jimmy Christopher murmured: "Good old dad!" and began to saw away at the window bars. The rasping of the saw was entirely drowned by the chorus of voices!

The priests looked up several times, but did not disturb the singers. And in less than fifteen minutes, Jimmy had two of the bars cut through. He squirmed through the window, dropped to the floor. And several of the singers, seeing him, involuntarily halted their song. This attracted the attention of the two priests, who turned their heads, saw Jimmy, and sprang to their feet.

One of them ran toward a small gong near the altar, with the intention of striking it. The other reached out his bloody hands, seized a long, sacrificial knife which was still red from the last victim's blood. He leaped from the altar and raced across the room past the cages at Jimmy. He brandished the knife wildly, and his eyes blazed with a murderous, fanatical fury.

Jimmy Christopher's automatic sprang into his hand like a live thing, and barked twice. He shot first at the priest who was raising the baton to strike the gong; then at the second one, who had the knife. Both shots were aimed for the heart, and both went home. The first white-robed devotee of the Aztec cult collapsed over the brass gong without striking it. The second fell literally at Jimmy's feet, and though he had a slug in his heart, he raised a hate-stained face, lifted his knife to slash. And in that moment death overtook him. He fell face down on the stone floor.

Jimmy rushed to the cage in which his father was crouching, and disregarding the shouts of the other prisoners he reached through the bars, clasped his father's hand.

"Dad!" he exclaimed, almost choking with emotion. "Good old dad! I'll have you out of here in no time!"

John Christopher clung to his son's hand for a moment, tears filming his eyes. Then he said huskily: "Jimmy, lad! How did you get here?"

The other prisoners were shouting: "Save us! Save us!" and

their voices reached a high pitch of frenzy. Jimmy had to raise his voice so as to be heard by his father.

"I failed, dad," he said. "I failed miserably. I had a chance to kill Montezuma, and didn't shoot because of a woman!" He spoke swiftly, relating the events that had brought him here, telling his father hour F-13 had died, and how the man had revealed his identity. As he spoke, Jimmy set to work on the bars of the cage with his saw.

John Christopher grasped his hand. "No, no, Jimmy. Leave me. There's something more important."

Jimmy Christopher gazed, uncomprehending at his father. "More important?"

John Christopher nodded. "F-13 and I were at the Texas border when we were captured. You know why we went there—an electro-chemist named George Powers claimed to know the secret of Montezuma's mysterious force."

"I know," said Jimmy. "He wrote to Washington, and Z-7 sent you and F-13 to interview him."

"That's right, son. Well, we were all captured—F-13, myself, and Powers, together with his wife and daughter. Powers is here, son, in the next room, with his family. *You've got to get him out of here, and learn what he knows!*"

"And leave you, dad?"

JOHN CHRISTOPHER gazed deeply into his son's eyes. "You're Operator 5, Jimmy, of the United States Intelligence. Forget that you are my son. Getting Powers out of here may mean the salvation of our country."

Thee other prisoners had grown quiet, watching these two. Perhaps they had realized that their shouts might attract guards.

In the comparative quiet, Jimmy said: "I'll get Powers, then come back for you, dad. We'll fight our way—"

John Christopher stopped him, shaking his head. "You can't do it, Jimmy. Look at the bars on this cage they're four times as thick as the bars on that window. It would take you an hour to cut through one of them, and a guard detail looks in here every hour. There's one due in a short while."

The older man was speaking urgently now, almost pleadingly. "The Powers family is in the next room, and the connecting door is open. It'll be an almost hopeless task to get them out as it is. But if you stop to saw these bars as well—no, Jimmy, you must leave me."

Jimmy's eyes were bitter, as they strayed to the poor, mangled remains of the dead man on the altar at the feet of the heathen god. "So they can offer your heart—?"

"Even that, Jimmy," John Christopher answered in a calm voice. "I am ready—in fact, I've been ready for a long time. Only, if you will, Jimmy, leave me that death's-head watch-charm of yours. Maybe I can break the capsule inside it, and spare myself and these others—" he motioned toward the other caged prisoners—"the—ordeal."

For a long time, Jimmy Christopher crouched beside that cage, fighting a terrific battle within himself, while his fingers toyed nervously with the death's-head charm on its chain. He knew very well what his father meant, and his eyes were bleak. He always carried that watch-charm with him. For within it, there reposed a silver, thin-walled capsule of *diphenolchlorasine*, a liquid which, upon being exposed to the action of the atmosphere, changed at once into a gas—a gas so volatile that it would cause instant death. By removing the capsule from the watch-charm and pinching it, Jimmy could at any time bring about the immediate death of everyone within a radius of fifty feet—including himself.

And his father was asking for this watch—charm now...!

Jimmy Christopher's pain-filled eyes sought those of his father. He was like a small child seeking guidance.

He asked in a thick, choked voice: "If *I* were in that cage, Dad, would—would you—leave me—to die?"

Quietly, with cool eyes steady, John Christopher nodded. Without hesitation he said:

"If our situations were reversed, I would, Jimmy. We mean much to each other—but think of the millions of fathers and sons and mothers who will be spared the pain of losing loved ones if you can only break the power of Montezuma!"

Suddenly, uttering a little choked cry, Jimmy tore the watch-charm from the chain, handed it to his father. Their hands met between the cage bars, clasped firmly. They avoided looking at each other.

"Right behind you," John Christopher said, "is the door to the room where Powers is held. Good-bye, son—and good luck to you!"

Blindly, Jimmy Christopher tore his hand from the older man's, turned and made his way, stumbling, across the chamber.

The other prisoners in their cages sensed that they were being left to their fate, and began to howl, shout and scream.

Jimmy Christopher hardly heard them. He pushed through the connecting door, entered the next room without looking back at his father—lest he weaken and return….

CHAPTER 5
UNMASKED!

THE ROOM Jimmy Christopher entered was much smaller than the other. It was lighted by only a single candle, which was burning very low.

Jimmy closed the connecting door, stared at the three occupants of the room. They were a man and two women, and they sat on the stone floor, looking at Jimmy in terror.

Jimmy said: "Have no fear. I am a friend."

He noted that each of the three was secured to the wall by a heavy chain about the right ankle, and that the three chains were all fastened to a single staple in the wall. If they wanted to walk they could probably walk two or three feet away from the corner in which they crouched, but no more.

The man was in his early fifties, gray-haired, with an absent look in his watery eyes. Jimmy assumed that this was George Powers, the electro-chemist. Next to him sat a plump lady with a tear-stained face. She was perhaps forty-eight or forty-nine. Beside her sat a girl, hardly more than nineteen or twenty. She was blonde, and pretty in a child-like sort of way, though tears had stained the white cheeks of her thin, almost elf-like face.

It was she who spoke first. "You—you are not from—Montezuma?"

Jimmy shook his head, knelt beside them. "I'll try to take you out of here—if you're willing to risk it," He turned to the man. "You are George Powers?"

The gray-haired man lifted vacant eyes to him. "Eh?" he asked in a cracked voice. "What's that you say? I'd like some tobacco for my pipe, young man. Do you know where my pipe is?"

Jimmy said impatiently: "Mr. Powers! I am going to take you out of here, to get you through the Aztec lines to Washington. Do you understand?" Powers gazed at him vacantly.

"Washington? I tell you, I want my pipe." He turned to the plump lady, said irritatedly: "Emma! Where is my pipe? You always used to get me my pipe."

There were tears in the plump lady's eyes. She said softly: "Yes, George, dear. I'll get your pipe—soon. Just have patience." She put a hand on Jimmy Christopher's arm. "Please," she begged. "He—he's sick. The shock of capture—" she threw a significant side glance at her husband—"he hasn't been quite right since we were brought here."

Jimmy nodded understandingly. "Once we get him out of here, he can be brought around. We'll get the best physicians in the world. The knowledge that is locked in his mind will save America." He turned to the girl. You are—?"

"His daughter," she answered. "Helen Powers. We were all caught together, with two agents—"

"I know," Jimmy said. He set to work briskly, examined

the chains about their ankles. Each was fastened with a large padlock.

Helen Powers said urgently: "Please, I don't know who you are, but we trust you. You must act quickly if we are to escape. Montezuma—" she lowered her eyes "is going to send for me in a few minutes."

Jimmy looked at her. "Why?"

She hesitated, blushed. She seemed fragile, delicate, with the slight tinge of red in her cheeks. Mrs. Powers answered for her. "Montezuma intends to—take Helen away from us. He has taken a fancy to her. He says he will share his empire with her!"

Jimmy whistled. Montezuma—infatuated with this slip of a girl!

Suddenly Helen Powers buried her face in her hands, and her little body was wracked with sobs. "I don't want to be an empress!" she blurted. "I'm afraid! Afraid of that terrible man!"

Jimmy was working swiftly with the padlocks. His mind and his heart were with John Christopher in the cage in the next room, but automatically he soothed the girl. "Don't worry. You'll be away from here before he sends for you."

The long, supple steel instrument with which Jimmy had been working on the old man's lock clicked it open, and the chain was off George Power's ankle. The other two padlocks yielded in short order, while the three watched him, two with suddenly reviving hope and the third with vacant interest.

AND AT that moment, disaster came to knock at the door. The heavy tread of footsteps sounded in the corridor outside. Helen Powers' face lost all its color. "They're coming!" she gasped.

71

George Powers displayed no especial interest, merely staring at the wall, vacantly. But Mrs. Powers began to sob quietly. Her hopes had been raised so high, only to be dashed.

But Jimmy Christopher acted swiftly, with quick decision. He stooped quickly, replaced the heavy chain about the older man's ankle, but without snapping the padlock. He did the same for the two women, then hurried to the far end of the room, crouched against the wall in the shadows where the light of the candle did not reach.

He was not a second too soon. The footsteps had stopped at the next room, and many voices were raised in excitement. They had discovered the dead bodies of the priests. This must be the guard detail that John Christopher had spoken of.

One voice, uttering hot, angry orders in Spanish, Jimmy recognized. It was that of Horgavo. He heard Horgavo say: "Send for more men. Place guards in every corridor. Operator 5 must not leave the palace. I will give twenty ounces of gold to the one who kills him!"

There was a mad marching and trampling of feet outside, and the connecting door opened. Horgavo peered in cautiously. His narrow eyes darted to the corner where the Powers family crouched, and his lips twisted in a smile. He stepped into the room, closing the door behind him. He paid no attention to the vacant-eyed scientist or his wife, but moved over to tower above the shrinking figure of the girl, Helen.

"I am glad that you are safe, Miss Powers," he said softly. "My master would have been very angry had anything happened to you."

Horgavo bent over her, leering. "The noble Montezuma has chosen you to be his lady. I hope that when you are empress you will not forget the humble Horgavo." He holstered his gun, produced a key from his pocket, and started to insert it in the padlock. "Now, you must come—"

He stopped abruptly as he heard Jimmy Christopher step out from the shadows. He straightened, turned, and his hand darted to the holstered pistol at his side.

Jimmy Christopher covered the distance between them in a quick leap, brought up his bunched fist to the point of the other's jaw. Horgavo's hand fell away empty from his holster, his eyes glazed, his knees buckled, and he collapsed to the floor.

George Powers' vacant eyes were fixed on the brightly uniformed, inert body. "I wonder," he cackled, "if he has a pipe on him?"

The two women gazed in terror.

Jimmy Christopher paid them no attention. Acting swiftly, he dragged the unconscious Horgavo over under the candle where the light was best.

"You ladies," he said, "had better turn your backs for a few minutes. Maybe we can squirm out of this." And he began to remove the uniform from the inert officer. As in a daze, Mrs. Powers and her daughter arose, turned away.

Jimmy Christopher's fingers worked with desperate speed. He got his own clothes off, squirmed into Horgavo's uniform. Then, while men stormed to and from in the corridor outside, while frantic orders were issued in hoarse voices, Operator 5 took from the inner lining of the coat he had discarded a flat leather case, which, when opened, revealed a number of tubes, and many small metal plates of various colors, set into slits in the case.

There was also a mirror and a small, flat battery which had been especially constructed at Jimmy Christopher's specifications to fit into the case. There was a small bulb fitted into the frame of the mirror, and when it was connected with the battery, this bulb gave off a powerful light through a small magnifying-glass set into the top. It furnished enough light for the delicate task Jimmy now undertook.

The tubes contained plastic material, tints and dyes. The small, metal plates were nose and cheek fillers, ear distorters, tooth coverings. In short, that case contained everything necessary for effecting a perfect-make-up....

NOW, WITH the mirror before him on its collapsible stand, illuminated by the magnifier-bulb, Jimmy Christopher's fingers fairly flew over his face. From time to time he stopped to examine Horgavo's features, and then he would continue with his work.

Seconds sped into minutes while the two women stood with their backs to him. And gradually, the coarse features of Horgavo began to take shape, superimposed upon the face of Operator 5. With exquisite skill, Jimmy Christopher spread his own nose, by means of two little plates inserted in the nostrils, so that it became the exact replica of the unconscious officer's. Using the plastic material, he created the effect of Horgavo's high cheek-bones. Then he used the tubes of tint to duplicate the officer's face coloring.

At last he was finished, and packed away the make-up case. He covered the unconscious man's body with his own discarded clothing, threw a grim smile at George Powers, who had been watching him listlessly, and got to his feet. Standing there in the dim light thrown by the candle, anyone would have sworn that he was an officer of Montezuma. He cleared his throat, and spoke: "You may turn around, now, ladies."

But his voice was not the voice of Jimmy Christopher. His marvelous ability had duplicated to the very slightest tone quality the voice of Horgavo!

Mrs. Powers and her daughter whirled, startled, and Helen Powers shrank away, uttering a little cry of terror. Her eyes jerked unbelievingly to the unconscious form of the officer on the floor. She had seen him knocked out, could not understand what had happened.

Jimmy said: "It's all right, Miss Powers. Your father was watching me. He will tell you that I am not Horgavo."

George Powers nodded, cackled. "Very clever young man. Very clever indeed. He ought to be an actor. But you shouldn't have hit that man so hard."

Jimmy stepped over to him, helped him to his feet. "Come on, Mr. Powers. We're going out through the front way."

Mrs. Powers gasped: "We'll be caught. We can't do that!"

Jimmy Christopher laughed bitterly. "Why should you be caught? You will be escorted out by the great Horgavo, the right-hand man of Montezuma. Come!"

He led them to the corridor door, flung it open, and stepped out....

This was the crucial moment. Back there in the dim light of the dungeon room, the two women had taken him for Horgavo. But the disguise had been hastily assumed; he had worked quickly, spurred by great necessity. It was possible that he had omitted some slight detail that would betray him at once to the soldiers, here, in the better light.

Jimmy kept his hand close to the holster, with his fingers taut. If his impersonation were discovered now, everything would be lost. He might kill half a dozen of these Aztec soldiers, but he could never hope to fight his way out of the palace with the Powers family.

Grimly he stood for a moment in the doorway while the eyes of several of the hurrying, excited soldiers rested on him. But they noticed nothing. Each of them saluted briskly as he passed. Jimmy heaved a sigh of relief, moved along the corridor, motioning to the Powers family to follow him. They moved along behind him nervously, the two women holding tight to each other's hands.

As they came abreast of the next door in the corridor, Jimmy Christopher halted a moment. His pulse was racing. In there was his father. Rescue of John Christopher had seemed impossible a little while ago.

But now...?

Major Horgavo, it seemed, was second in power only to Montezuma. Disguised as the major, was it not possible to effect his father's release too?

Jimmy turned abruptly, said to his wards: "Come in here with me!"

Grimly he pushed aside the guard who stood before the wide door, stepped into the sacrificial chamber in which his father was caged. A dozen soldiers were here now, and some of them were moving the bodies of the dead priests to one side. The prisoners in the cages were silent, staring in terror. They feared that the Aztecs would exact dreadful reprisals from them for the deaths of the priests.

Jimmy's eyes flicked to the cage where his father crouched. John Christopher had raised his eyes, was staring at him, but without any hint of recognition.

A JUNIOR officer, who was in command of the detail, approached, clicked his heels smartly together, and saluted. "Your orders," he said, "have been carried out, major. Guards have been posted everywhere. The American Secret Service man cannot escape from the palace without being seen. All sentries outside have been doubled, and warned to be on the lookout for him."

He spoke in Spanish, and Jimmy answered him in the same language, mimicking to perfection the thick, guttural speech of Horgavo.

"It is well. Go now, and get me the key to these cages."

The junior officer hesitated, looked puzzled. "But you know, sir, that only Montezuma has the key to these cages. Montezuma himself chooses the next victims for the sacrifices."

Jimmy's blood suddenly ran cold. His hopes of rescuing his father by means of this disguise had been high. But he had not foreseen this.

He saw John Christopher gazing at the Powers family in

hopeless dejection. He understood that his father was thinking that there was no more hope. The sight of Horgavo, in charge of Powers could mean only one thing to the older man—that Jimmy had failed in his attempt to rescue them, and that everything was lost.

Jimmy Christopher said to the young officer in Spanish: "Leave me here. Take your men out for a few moments."

The officer saluted, turned and gave reluctant orders to his men, who began to file out. The lieutenant followed, saying, puzzledly:

"I obey, Major Horgavo, but I do not understand?"

"It is not necessary that you understand," Jimmy broke in coldly. He waited until the door had closed behind the last of them, and then hurried over to his father's cage.

"Dad!" he exclaimed. "Didn't you recognize me?"

John Christopher swung startled eyes to his son. "Jimmy! You! I—I thought you had been caught or—killed in there!"

"I'm going to get you out of here, dad, while I have the chance. These others, too!"

John Christopher's voice took on an edge of steel. "No. You'd only be caught. There's too much to risk. Go now. Take the Powers family out of here. Get Powers to Washington."

"Look at him, dad," Jimmy interrupted. "He's lost his mind from shock. Shall I have you to die for the sake of that?"

"You know very well it's only a temporary shock, Jimmy. Once he's out of here, in the care of competent doctors, he'll recover his mind, and give us the secret that will save America—the secret of Montezuma's mysterious force!"

Jimmy lowered his eyes rebelliously.

John Christopher said firmly but gently: "I know it's hard for you, Jimmy. But remember, I've got that watch-charm of yours. Death will not be hard for me...."

Jimmy sighed; "Good-bye, dad," he choked, and turned to the Powers family. "Come!" he ordered, and stumbled from the room.

Out in the corridor, he recovered his poise, said to the young officer who was looking at him suspiciously: "The prisoner on the third cage to the left must not be harmed in any way. He is the father of that gringo, Operator 5, and will be a valuable hostage in case we do not recapture the son."

The young officer saluted and Jimmy motioned to the Powers family to follow him. They had not said a word all this time, but followed Jimmy docilely.

Now Jimmy led the way up along a steep stone staircase that must be the mate of the one he had descended. Helen Powers, walking close beside him on the stairs, plucked at his sleeve timidly. "W-where are you taking us?"

Jimmy told her grimly: "We are going to walk out through the front entrance. Say nothing. Leave all the talking to me. And see if you can keep your father quiet."

They reached the top of the long flight of stairs, came out into the main hallway. Here there were many uniformed men, all armed. Every nook and cranny of the palace was being searched for Operator 5.

Jimmy led the way in the direction of the wide entrance, before which a detail of armed men was drawn up. Soldiers

TIM DONOVAN

saluted him respectfully all the way along the hall. He was even imitating Horgavo's manner of walking.

Helen Powers, alongside him, whispered: "Please God you can carry it through!"

"If we can only get safely outside."

Jimmy said, "I can commandeer one of the palace cars. We'll say I'm talking you to other quarters at the command of Montezuma. We—"

80

He suddenly ceased talking, stopped short with a hand on Helen Powers' arm. A door at the left of the corridor had opened, and Dolores, the daughter of Montezuma, stood framed in the doorway.

Her dark, imperious eyes returned Jimmy Christopher's stare. Her red lips curved in a cold smile. "You do not salute me, Major Horgavo?" she asked icily.

Helen Powers barely restrained a gasp of dismay, while her father and mother huddled close to Jimmy.

Jimmy left them standing there, came over close to Dolores, saluting. "A thousand pardons, princess," he said. His eyes were gleaming with a sudden, bold plan. "Something of grave importance has arisen. May I see you alone for a moment?"

She studied him a moment, and her eyes dropped to his right hand. There, exposed to her gaze, a peculiar grayish birthmark. It was in the shape of an American eagle, and it shone, grayish under the red cuff of the bright uniform. Jimmy Christopher had carried that strange birthmark with him all his life, had become

so used to it that he forgot it most of the time; forgot that it was noticeable to other people.

Now he looked into Dolores dark eyes, saw that she was smiling cruelly.

"You," she announced sternly, "are not Major Horgavo. You are Operator 5!"

THE HALL was teeming with armed servants of Montezuma. Dolores had only to raise her voice, and a hundred men would swarm about Jimmy Christopher and his wards, each one eager to earn the reward of gold offered for his death. She was aware of this, and she took a crude delight in the situation.

But Jimmy Christopher gave her no opportunity to summon help. He had seen recognition in her eyes even before she spoke; and he acted swiftly, surely. His right hand slipped inside his bright red tunic to his mechanical pencil. His thumbnail flipped up the small metal plate covering the top. This plate opened on a hinge, exposing a grayish powder that nestled in the receptacle where one usually carries spare leads.

Jimmy dipped his thumbnail in the powder, then withdrew his hand, leaving the pencil in his pocket. The whole thing was so swiftly done that Dolores noticed nothing until Jimmy reached out, took her arm. She was just saying: "You are not going to escape, Operator 5. I think I shall enjoy your company for a short time—and then I shall enjoy even more watching you die—"

She broke off, startled, as Jimmy, leaning over her, raked his thumbnail down the flesh of her soft, white arm. She winced with pain as the sharp nail tore the skin of her arm, making a bloody furrow.

The powder on Jimmy's thumbnail entered the wound. It was a chemical that Operator 5 had developed in his own laboratory in New York. The few grains on his thumbnail were sufficient to induce a coma lasting for several hours. It consisted of a mixture of urethane, scopolamine and ethyl chloride, delicately balanced so as to form the most powerful anesthetic known to man.

Its effect on Dolores was immediate. Her whole body stiffened, her eyes glazed, and the words she had been about to utter died on her lips. She would have collapsed if Jimmy had not placed an arm about her waist, half carried her into the room from which she had appeared. The whole thing had been done so swiftly that, to those passing in the hall, nothing extraordinary seemed to have taken place. Indeed, no one looked very closely, for they preferred to keep a good distance from Horgavo and the daughter of Montezuma.

Jimmy lost no time. He laid the unconscious princess on the floor, sprang across the room and yanked down one of the silken drapes hanging over the window. While Helen Powers with her father and mother waited breathless just outside the door, Jimmy wrapped the drape completely around the princess, lifted her dead weight up in his arms, and strode out into the hall.

"Follow me," he said to them, and led the way out through the broad main entrance, past the lined-up guards. A junior officer saw him, said obsequiously: "Can I help you carry that—burden, sir?"

Jimmy shook his head. "No. But you can get me a car and a chauffeur. I must take these people away at once, by order of the emperor."

The officer saluted, left. In less than five minutes, a big car pulled up at the entrance, driven by a gaudily uniformed Indian chauffeur. The officer was riding the running board.

"Do you wish an escort, Major Horgavo?" he asked. "This gringo, Operator 5 is loose, and there may be danger."

"Never mind," Jimmy Christopher said. "I can take care of him." He bundled the unconscious princess into the car, had the door open for Helen Powers and her father and mother. Then he closed the door, went around in front and got in with the chauffeur.

He said to the driver in Spanish: "Just a minute," and took from his pocket a small notebook and his pencil. While the officer waited at attention, he wrote upon a page of the notebook:

> Emperor Montezuma:
>
> I have your daughter with me. If any harm should come to my father while he is in your hands, I swear that Dolores will never return to you. If you attempt to use your explosive force to prevent our escape, your daughter will perish with us.
> —Operator 5.

Jimmy Christopher tore the page from the notebook, folded it and gave it to the officer.

"See that this is delivered at once to the emperor," he said.

The officer took it, bowing. "It shall be done, major." He watched while the chauffeur got the car in motion. "Drive to the flying field," Jimmy directed.

AS THE car rolled away from the palace, Jimmy glanced back into the rear, to see Helen Powers supporting the inert body of the princess, still wrapped in the drape. George Powers and his wife were sitting in the two folding-seats. Powers was listless, while his plump wife was nervously tearing a handkerchief to shreds.

Jimmy faced forward again, staring out into the night along the wash of the car's powerful headlights. He glanced at his wrist watch. It was eleven o'clock; only two fleeting hours had passed since he had landed here, a prisoner. Now he was riding in an imperial car which had the right of way over all other traffic; he was taking away, with him the one man who might be able to reveal the secret of the mysterious force which enabled the Aztecs to decimate United States troops; he was abducting the daughter of Montezuma. But he had a heavy heart. His father....

The car came in sight of the flying field. Jimmy's blood raced. This was going to be a crucial moment. Was there a plane available that could carry five people—and could he get it?

An official came out of the operations building, bowed low when he saw the man he thought to be Major Horgavo descend from the car. Jimmy asked brusquely in Spanish: "Have you a large plane available? One that will accommodate four besides the pilot?"

Elation glowed in Jimmy's eyes as the official replied obsequiously: "But yes, señor. We have a large transcontinental plane that we captured from the gringos only yesterday. It is all ready in the hangar. I can have a pilot—"

"I will fly it myself," Jimmy announced.

The official raised his eyebrows. "I did not know, Major Horgavo, that you could—"

Jimmy said coldly, in the tone which he was almost certain the major would employ: "There are many things you do not know. Be careful that your lack of knowledge does not cause you—unhappiness."

The official squirmed. "But I meant nothing at all, Major! I am only too glad to serve you. I will have the plane ready in ten minutes."

"Five minutes," Jimmy said firmly. "Otherwise—"

"But of course, señor," the official agreed hastily. "It shall be done as you say!" He hurried away.

Operator 5 returned to the car, and with the aid of Helen Powers and her mother, he got out the bundled form of Dolores, placed her on the ground. George Powers got out, stared around him vacantly.

"Are we going to take a ride in a plane?" he asked with sudden interest. "Do you think I'll be able to get a pipe and some tobacco where we're going?"

Jimmy Christopher sighed, turned away from him. "You may go," he told the chauffeur. "Leave the car here. You need not return to the palace. You may have the rest of the night off."

The Indian chauffeur got out of the car with alacrity. "Gracias, señor!" he said, saluting, and hurried away toward a troop-truck which was just ready to return to the city.

Jimmy, watching him go, said to Helen Powers: "He won't report back for duty till tomorrow morning—and Montezuma may not learn for hours that we have commandeered the plane."

He donned the helmet and goggles which one of the mechanics brought him, helped Powers and the two women to put on similar equipment. Then he motioned to two men who stood nearby to carry the princess, and started across toward the huge passenger plane which was being wheeled out of a hangar at the other end of the field.

The Powers family followed him.... The rest was easy....

CHAPTER 6
SLAVERY OR DEATH!

NEWARK AIRPORT was a bedlam of excitement. Bright incandescents made daylight of the field. Planes were taking off one after the other, each with a full quota of passengers.

Near one edge of the field, a squad of Secret Service men were anxiously watching a huge transport that had banked into the wind and was settling to a perfect landing. Brakes squealed as the plane taxied toward them.

The Secret Service men swarmed about it, while several of them made sure that no unauthorized person approached. They all seemed nervous, high-strung, as if they expected trouble.

From the pilot's compartment of the plane emerged Operator 5. He had not yet removed the uniform or makeup of Major Horgavo, and he had to identify himself to the Secret Service operatives. He shook hands with B-6, a small, wiry man, who was in charge of the squad. "Why are all these planes taking off?" Jimmy asked. "The airline seems to be having a rush of business."

B-6 nodded jerkily. "People are fleeing the city," he replied in terse, clipped accents. "Montezuma is striking here. That's why

Z-7 hurried to New York, and wired you to fly directly here to meet him. He's waiting for you at Address Y." B-6 extended a yellow sheet. "Here's a message from Z-7. He instructed me to deliver it to you as soon as you landed."

Jimmy took the message, and his eyes clouded as he read:

OPERATOR 5—MEN WOMEN DYING BY EXPLOSION IN STREETS OF NEW YORK... MONTEZUMA DEMANDS UNCONDITIONAL SURRENDER... CLAIMS HE CAN DESTROY NEW YORK CITY WITHIN TWENTY-FOUR HOURS... WE CANNOT LOCATE HEADQUARTERS OF AGENTS HERE... MUST ACT QUICKLY OR POPULAR PANIC WILL FORCE PRESIDENT TO CAPITULATE... RUSH POWERS TO MEDICAL CENTER FOR ATTENTION... SEE ME AT ONCE AT ADDRESS Y... Z-7....

Jimmy crushed the paper in his hand. He spoke swiftly. "I've got George Powers in the plane, with his wife and daughter. The Aztec princess, Dolores, is also in there, being watched by Tim Donovan."

He added in explanation, as he saw B-6's surprised look: "I picked Tim up at Fort Sam Houston on the way up. Now the first thing to be done is to get Powers into the hands of competent physicians—"

"We've arranged that," B-6 told him. "We have half a dozen specialists at the Medical Center, waiting for him right now— the biggest men in the country. If they can't do anything with him, nobody can. There's even a doctor from Washington, who just flew in by plane."

"All right," Jimmy said. "You take care of him. I'll take care of Powers' wife and daughter. Have two cars ready—one for Powers, and another for the two women. Tim and I will take care of the Princess Dolores."

He watched B-6 walk over to the plane to take charge of the scientist, then he entered the operations-office and used the phone to arrange for a room for Helen Powers and her mother at the Beacon Hotel which was often used by Intelligence....

When Jimmy came out of the operations—office, he saw Powers being driven off in a car with a guard of Intelligence men. At his direction, B-6 ordered another car to take Helen and her mother to the Beacon; then the wiry little agent returned and reported. "Your roadster is here, too, Operator 5. Z-7 ordered one of the men to drive it out for you. It's parked back of the operations office."

"Splendid!" Jimmy retorted. "Have the roadster brought here."

B-6 left to execute the order, and Jimmy went over to the plane, entered the passenger compartment. He found Tim Donovan grimly guarding the Princess Dolores, who sat stiffly disdainful. When Jimmy climbed in, her dark eyes flashed with momentary fear.

"What are you going to do with me?" she queried huskily.

Jimmy said gently: "You will not be harmed, princess. Come with me."

He turned and led the way out. The princess' eyes flashed, but she followed, accompanied by Tim Donovan.

AS JIMMY CHRISTOPHER drove swiftly toward New York City, his mind reverted to the crisis facing the nation. B-6's sketchy information had been filled out by the messages which Jimmy had gotten over the phone. All of New York, he learned, was under martial law. People did not dare to leave their homes, for the exploding death struck everywhere. And even their homes were not safe, it appeared, for men had been exploded within theatres, offices and residences. Montezuma's mysterious force could reach everywhere, and he was spreading terror and demoralization throughout New York.

Operator 5's eyes scanned with grim bitterness the motor trucks full of soldiers which they passed on the road. The mobilizing of these men was only a futile gesture—for Montezuma could destroy them in a moment, just as he had destroyed others. These soldiers were contingents of the National Guard, which had been called to the colors overnight. It was the only thing that the government could think of doing—well knowing the futility of mobilizing troops that could be wiped out by the enemy at will; yet—what else was there to do…?

The soldiers in the trucks were not laughing and singing as the National Guard usually do when on their way to training camps in the summer. This was no pleasant two weeks of training and target practice that they were going to; at any moment, without warning, they might be destroyed in a dreadful, inexplicable manner. Their faces were very somber, gray.…

At the Holland Tunnel, Jimmy was stopped by a lieutenant of the regular army in charge of a detail of men. Every car was being examined. Jimmy Christopher had removed his gaudy uniform, but he still kept the make-up on his face. He produced credentials showing that he was George Wakely, of the Department of Justice. The lieutenant at once stepped aside.

As they drove through the tunnel, the princess Dolores fidgeted in her seat between Jimmy and Tim Donovan. Finally she spoke. "Where are you taking me, Operator 5?"

"To the apartment of a very good friend of mine," Jimmy told her. "A young lady who will take excellent care of you. We're not going to any of the regular Intelligence offices because I'm afraid that your father's agents will already be watching those spots. Where I am taking you, you will be er—safe!"

Tim exclaimed: "We're not going to Diane's apartment, are we Jimmy?"

Operator 5 nodded. "I need an unofficial place. The princess is an unofficial prisoner. Diane, being a newspaper reporter, and not an Intelligence agent, will not be suspected by Montezuma's agents."

AT THE New York end of the tunnel, Jimmy swung north to Gramercy Park, drew up before a small, two-story brownstone house. With himself on one side and Tim on the other, the princess was brought up the short flight of stone steps. Before they could touch the bell, the door was opened by a trim, chestnut-haired young lady whose softly modeled face reflected deep anxiety as she gazed at the princess, at Jimmy, and finally at Tim Donovan.

"Hello, Tim," she said. "I'm so glad you're safe." She looked questioningly at Operator 5, not recognizing him in his disguise. Then she glanced once more at Tim Donovan, a question in her eyes. "W-where is Jimmy? He phoned me from the airport that he was coming here with you—"

She was gazing directly at Jimmy, but seeing only the gross-featured face of Horgavo which the make-up showed.

Operator 5 chuckled, and Tim burst out laughing. "I fooled you that time Di—I didn't think you'd fall for it!"

Tim Donovan took the princess by the arm, escorted her into the house.

Jimmy walked ahead with Diane, explaining to her swiftly what had taken place in Mexico City. "As long as we can keep Dolores out of the way, Di," he finished, "Dad may be comparatively safe. Montezuma won't dare to harm him for fear of reprisal. Of course, he doesn't know that we aren't capable of the same kind of cruelty that he indulges in. Men like him can't understand anyone who is different from themselves."

Diane said eagerly: "I'll put her in the spare bedroom. There are bars on the window, because it's a ground floor. She won't be able to get away."

Jimmy nodded. "And stay here every minute of the time, Di. If you see anyone or anything suspicious in the neighborhood, phone me at Dad's house. If I'm not there, talk to the man who answers the phone. He'll be someone you can trust."

When they had gotten the princess safely in the spare room, Operator 5 and Tim Donovan prepared to take their leave. Diane went to the door with them. Her face bore a troubled expression. "Jimmy," she said! "I'm—I'm afraid for the country. Terrible things are happening. Tonight the entire audience of the International Theater and two other theaters were killed in

92

their seats. They exploded—" she snapped her fingers—"poof! Just like that! The theater was like a—like a charnel house! I went over there to cover the story for the Amalgamated, and it was—beyond description. No one can understand how it was done."

Jimmy soothed her. "If we can only bring George Powers back to sanity, we'll know the answer. He pressed Diane's hand. "We're off, Di. Remember, stay here every minute. Come on, Tim…!"

OUTSIDE, TIM scrambled into the seat beside Operator 5. As the powerful Diesel engine purred to life, and the car slipped effortlessly away from the curb, Tim asked: "Where to now, Jimmy?"

"We're going to Dad's house," Operator 5 told the lad. "Z-7 is waiting for us there. Then we'll phone the Medical Center, and see what progress they've made with Powers."

Four times they were stopped on their trip, forced to show their credentials. The city was in the grip of a reign of terror.…

Jimmy swung north on Fifth Avenue, drove to a quiet residential street in the East Forties. Here was the unpretentious brownstone house which was John Christopher's home in New York. It had also been entered among the official addresses of the United States Intelligence as "Address Y." Jimmy had a laboratory here, and did much work in this house. It was here that he had perfected his anesthetic powder that he had used with such success on the Princess Dolores.

Jimmy Christopher, with the caution that had many times saved himself and Tim Donovan from death, did not drive up directly to the house. He slowed up upon turning the corner, observed the street keenly. It was deserted, as were all the other streets of the city. He drove past slowly, blew his horn twice, and watched the window on the ground floor.

In a moment, a face appeared at that window—the face of Z-7, Jimmy's chief. Z-7 lowered the shade, then raised it—the signal that the coast was clear. Then his face disappeared.

JIMMY PULLED in close to the opposite curb, preparing to make a complete turn and park before the building. But at that moment, a man darted out from a doorway near by, ran up close to the car. The man was swarthy, might have been a Latin American; but he might also have been a Mexican Indian.

Jimmy's hand involuntarily strayed toward his shoulder holster, and his eyes narrowed. But the man made no threatening moves. Instead he said, speaking rapidly in Spanish, and looking right past Tim at Jimmy:

"Do not go into that house, major. In five minutes the explosive death will be directed against it!"

For a moment, Jimmy had forgotten that he still retained makeup that duplicated the features of Major Horgavo. Now, suddenly, the full import of the man's words struck home. *In five minutes, everybody within Address Y would be destroyed!*

Jimmy saw that Tim Donovan's puzzled face was directed at the man, and he gripped the lad's hand before he could say anything that would give the game away.

Jimmy said sternly: "Who ordered this destruction?"

The man appeared nonplussed. "Why, major, you yourself ordered it, only a half hour ago, as soon as you arrived in New

York. I thought that you were here to see that your orders are carried out."

Jimmy thought quickly. *Horgavo in New York!* It meant that the Aztec invaders must have removed their headquarters from Mexico City. Horgavo could have flown here as well as Jimmy had. This was an opportunity to discover where the major was holed up. Five minutes to go. One was elapsed already.

Jimmy spoke swiftly, mimicking Horgavo's imperious tones: "You must be mistaken. Where was I when I ordered this?"

"Why, major," the man answered puzzled, "you were in the big house on the river—secret headquarters. You even gave me the address yourself!"

Jimmy thought quickly, while Tim Donovan sat tense, not understanding the Spanish, but realizing that something vital was in the wind. Horgavo must have discovered the secret of Address Y from some other agent whom he had tortured as F-3 had been tortured. Even now, Z-7 was in that house. With the shrewd chief of Intelligence dead, the whole service would he crippled for hours.

Jimmy said crisply in Spanish: "I wish to change my mind. I wish to countermand the order to direct the explosive death against that house. Cancel the order!"

The man stared at him suspiciously. "You know that cannot be done, major. The instruments have been set at the house on the river. You oet them yourself. The explosion will take place unless you yourself telephone to change the order. And—" he glanced at his watch—"there are but three minutes left!"

Jimmy Christopher said, very low: "I see." At the same time

his hand darted out past Tim's astonished face, in a lightning quick, stiff-fingered jab that caught the swarthy man at a point just beneath the Adam's apple. The man's eyes bulged, his mouth dropped open, and he collapsed to the pavement, writhing in agony.

Jimmy exclaimed: "Watch him, Tim!" and frantically punched his horn in a raucous summons. He turned his head as he did so, watching the window of the brownstone house. A face appeared there, and Jimmy thrust open the door of his car, sped across the street....

"Come out!" he shouted "Come out! Danger in there!"

The face at the open window was that of Z-7. The chief of Intelligence saw Jimmy gesticulating, but did not recognize Operator 5 behind the gross features of Horgavo. Z-7 frowned, thinking, perhaps, that it was some sort of trick to lure him into the open. He stepped back frown the window as Jimmy raced toward the house, and in a moment his hand appeared with an automatic.

THERE WAS, perhaps, only a minute or a minute and a half to spare. Jimmy Christopher acted like lightning, with the well-trained coördination of mind and muscle that had helped him in many a crisis in the past.

His right hand moved with eye-defying speed, came away from his shoulder holster with his own automatic; and before Z-7 could take aim, Jimmy Christopher's pistol had barked a single shot. The slug went true to its mark, struck Z-7's automatic, sent it spinning from his numbed hand.

And in a bound Jimmy Christopher was up the three steps of the stoop, calling frantically:

"Z-7! It's Operator 5! Come out of there—through the window! There's no time to lose!"

Z-7 looked out, his face pale, puzzled. He started to say: "Op—?"

But Jimmy did not let him finish. He reached over, grasped Z-7 by the sleeve, yanked powerfully. Z-7 lost his balance, came tumbling over the windowsill. Jimmy let him fall to the pavement, then leaped over the railing down beside him. Z-7 was struggling to his knees when Jimmy landed next to him, gripped him about the waist, raised him to his right shoulder and ran across the street.

Z-7 gasped: "Wait—what—?"

Jimmy said: "It's Operator 5, Z-7. Montezuma is going to send his exploding death into that house in less than a minute!"

Z-7 gasped: "My God! There's someone else in there—Yes! He was reporting—"

His words were cut off by the sound of a terrific, dull detonation emanating from the interior. Something like a cold draft of air pressed around them, and Jimmy suddenly found it hard to breath. He staggered to the opposite curb, let Z-7 rise to his feet. Then he looked toward the house. Every pane of glass in the brownstone house was shattered. Bits of clothing and torn flesh came catapulting through the open window from which Jimmy had dragged his chief.

Z-7 groaned: "Y-8! That's the end of him!" His face was

The pavement was littered with
wreckage, flesh, and bones!

purple with the effort of breathing. It was as if the air in the neighborhood had suddenly become polluted....

Immediately to the left of the brownstone house was an empty lot; but on the right was another building, also of brownstone, and this one seemed also to have suffered from the detonation, but not to the same extent. For the glass windows were also shattered, and a man and a woman came running from it, clutching at their throats as if to tear something dreadful away from them. Out on the sidewalk, they could run no more. They both dropped, writhed, and then stiffened, lay still.

Jimmy had been breathing in deep lungfuls of air. Now, suddenly, breathing seemed to become easier. In a moment it became normal. Jimmy left Z-7, crossed the street to the two prostrate bodies. He knelt beside them. Both were dead....

He looked up to find Z-7 and Tim Donovan beside him, staring down at the disfigured faces of the man and the woman. It seemed that their veins had burst, for their faces were clotted with blood, their eyes bulging, their tongues hanging from their mouths. They had both died in exactly the same way.

Z-7 said: "They were choked, somehow!"

Jimmy shook his head. "No, Z-7, they weren't choked. It's the same sort of death as killed our troops, as killed Y-8 in there. They exploded. Only the process wasn't completed with them for some reason, and they didn't die immediately. Perhaps the attack was concentrated on Dad's house, here, and they only got the excess."

Tim Donovan was staring about him, wide-eyed. "Gee, Jimmy, is it a sort of gas?"

"No, Tim, it isn't a gas. It is something far more deadly. Let's get hold of that fellow that warned us. He knows a lot, and we'll make him talk!"

Jimmy raced across the significantly empty street. Not even the sound of the explosion had brought anybody out—so great was the fear of the public. And that fear was very well based indeed, as the bodies of the man and woman on the pavement testified....

The swarthy man was just scrambling to his knees as Jimmy got across the street. He saw Jimmy coming, snarled, and his hand went to his armpit. Jimmy still had his automatic in his hand, and snapped a shot that caught the other in the right shoulder. The swarthy man's hand fell away from his holster, and he reeled against Jimmy's car.

Operator 5, with Tim Donovan at his side, came up to the man, caught him as he was about to fall. He looked up at Operator 5 with hate-filled eyes, gasped: "You—you are not Major Horgavo!"

Jimmy shook his head. "You are going to tell us everything you know about this explosive death, do you understand? Do you want to talk now, or shall I take you where you will be made to talk?"

The man winced with the pain of his wounded shoulder, whispered: "I will —"

He seemed to slump, but in a moment he straightened up, pushed Jimmy away from him. He wavered on his feet. He was holding a small white pellet in his hand. Operator 5 leaped toward him, but it was too late. The man lifted it to his mouth, swallowed it.

His lips twisted in a ghastly smile. In Spanish he said: "You cannot make—me talk—anymore. I—have been faithful to my emperor!" His body was suddenly convulsed in agony; he slumped to the pavement.

Jimmy bent beside him, heard him murmur through froth-flecked lips: "I—pay the penalty—of failure. I go to the bosom—of Huitzilopochtli!" And the man was dead....

Jimmy arose slowly, gazed somberly at Z-7 and at Tim Donovan. "At least," Jimmy said, "he died bravely. But I hope there are not many more like him in the service of Montezuma!"

CHAPTER 7
THE ROAD TO HELL

JIMMY CHRISTOPHER, with Tim Donovan and Z-7 in the car, drove uptown to the Medical Center.

At One Hundred and Sixty-eighth Street, Jimmy swung the roadster left, in through the wide gate leading to the grounds on which were erected the dozen or so buildings that comprised the huge institution.

They went up in the elevator to the ninth floor, where a dozen of the most eminent physicians in the country were gathered in the consultation room adjoining the chamber where George Powers was resting.

Dr. Angus Maynard, the head of the psychiatric department of the biggest hospital in the city, was presiding. In answer to

Jimmy Christopher's terse question, Dr. Maynard replied: "It is our opinion, young man, that the patient suffers from a trauma of the brain. That, of course, is a very general diagnosis. For more definite findings, it will be necessary to subject him to a series of tests to ascertain the extent to which his coördinative faculties—"

Jimmy Christopher interrupted him. "How long will these tests take that you propose?"

Dr. Maynard raised his eyebrows. "In cases such as these, young man, we cannot hasten things. I have often kept a patient under observation for as long as ten weeks—"

Jimmy Christopher heaved a deep sigh, cast a significant glance at Z-7 who had remained in the background, standing near the door with Tim Donovan.

"If you don't mind, doctor," Jimmy broke in, "I should like to talk to Powers myself. Perhaps I can extract some information from him without waiting ten weeks. The entire nation may well be destroyed while you conduct your tests!"

Doctor Maynard smiled in superior fashion. "The layman," he said indulgently, "never appreciates the problems which face the physician—"

"Pardon me, doctor," Jimmy said softly, "it so happens that I hold a degree of Doctor of Medicine myself. I studied under Prague and Liegnitz. If you will permit me—" he bowed to the assembled physicians—"to cut the red tape with which you have surrounded your profession!"

He stepped toward the connecting door which led to Powers' room. One of the other physicians, a Doctor Cabello, to whom

Jimmy had been introduced among others, hurried toward him, gripped his arm: "You mustn't go in there, young man! We are leaving the patient in strict solitude for three hours, after which we shall conduct further tests. If you disturb his rest now, you will ruin the tests!" Doctor Cabello was tall, thin, with piercing black eyes that commanded attention.

His fingers on Jimmy's arm felt strong as iron.

Jimmy Christopher said quietly: "I am sorry, Doctor Cabello, but Mr. Power's rest *must* be disturbed. This is an emergency."

Cabello shrugged. "Then I wash my hands of the whole affair. I will have nothing further to do with it." He turned to the other physicians. "Good day, gentlemen!" He bowed, stalked from the room.

Jimmy frowned, turned the knob, and entered the bedchamber of George Powers. Inside, he stopped stock-still, gazing at the motionless form on the white, clean bed. George Powers was dead. The needle of a hypodermic syringe had been thrust through his eye and had pierced his brain. He had died, bloodlessly, while asleep. Even in death his countenance was vacuous, peaceful. But he would never reveal the secret of Montezuma's mysterious force to anyone....

Jimmy Christopher swung about, thrust back into the consultation room again. He snapped at the astounded physicians: "Powers is dead—murdered! Who was with him last?"

Dr. Maynard stammered: "Why—why—we all were there. Dr. Cabello suggested that Powers be given an opiate so that he could rest. I filled the hypodermic, and Dr. Cabello administered it. I—"

Jimmy did not wait for him to finish. He lunged past Dr. Maynard, tore through the door into the corridor, with Tim Donovan and Z-7 following him. The white-tiled corridor was empty except for a neatly uniformed nurse who gazed in wonder at the two men and the boy who had barged out of the consultation room. Jimmy Christopher seized her arm, demanded: "Did you see a tall, thin man come out of here just now?"

The nurse nodded, bewildered. "Yes. A tall thin man just went down in the elevator."

Jimmy turned from her, to face Z-7 and Doctor Maynard, who had come out after them. "How long have you known Doctor Cabello?"

"I had never met him before," Doctor Maynard confessed. "In fact, I never heard of him as a specialist. But he came here with a letter signed by someone in the office of the Secretary of State. I thought he was a government doctor."

Operator 5's eyes met those of Z-7, and his lips formed one word: "Forgery!" He said aloud to Doctor Maynard: "Thank you, sir. I think there's no further use in our staying here." He glanced at Z-7 who nodded, and led the way to the elevator.

Downstairs, in the roadster, Tim Donovan rubbed his freckled nose in puzzlement. "Who was that Cabello guy, Jimmy?"

Jimmy Christopher explained dully: "He must be an agent of Montezuma. He came here with a forged letter from the office of the Secretary of State. Montezuma is making sure that we don't learn the secret of his mysterious power!"

"Which means," said Z-7 bitterly, "that we are back just where we started."

THE OLD Beacon Hotel on Fifty-ninth Street, was a super-annuated structure that would long since have been torn down had it not been for the financial support accorded it by the United States Intelligence Service.

The rental paid by the Intelligence Bureau for the fifteenth floor alone, was enough to defray the operating costs of the entire undertaking. The proprietor of the Beacon Hotel was a retired Intelligence Agent, and he knew how to render exactly the service required.

Here, on the fifteenth floor, many strange things had taken place that had never seen the light of day, never been reported in any newspaper. Here men from all over the world had sold secrets vital to the safety of the United States. To this hotel had come, from time to time, freelance spies with information to sell, inventors with ideas for destroying whole armies of the enemy in case of war. Intelligence agents were always on hand to interview them, to make deals, to investigate the worth of the things that were offered for sale.

Now the fifteenth floor of the Beacon Hotel played host to two women, fugitive from a ruthless invader. And it was to the Beacon Hotel that a young, keen-eyed man, accompanied by a freckled boy, came. At the desk the young man said to the desk clerk: "May I see Mr. Zilder, please?"

"Mr. Zilder?" the clerk asked. "What room is he in, sir?"

"1501," said the young man. "You might tell him that I come from Mr. Frost."

"Ah, yes; Mr. Frost. You mean Mr. Frost the architect?"

"No. Mr. Frost, the linguist."

The clerk was satisfied. "You wish to give Mr. Zilder a number, sir?"

"Yes," said the keen-eyed young man. "Tell him that Operator 5 is here."

"Yes, sir," said the clerk, suddenly deferential. "You may go right up, sir. Mr. Zilder is expecting you. It will not even be necessary to announce you."

Jimmy Christopher thanked the clerk, winked at Tim Donovan, and led the way to the elevator. At the fifteenth floor, Jimmy Christopher and Tim made their way down the corridor to 1501, and knocked at the door. It was opened in a moment by a man in a green eyeshade, who nodded a greeting, let them through. The room was equipped with a battery of telephones, and two teletype machines. A dozen agents were at work here, taking messages as fast as they came in.

The man in the green eyeshade said: "This way, Operator 5," and led the way through a connecting door into another room. Here there were filing cabinets reaching up to the ceiling, and more agents were busy cataloging information. They passed through this room into another, and here the man in the green eyeshade left them alone with the man who was sitting before the big battered desk. The man was Z-7….

He arose, shook hands with Jimmy Christopher, then with Tim Donovan.

Jimmy Christopher asked crisply: "Have you checked on all those locations I gave you, Chief?"

Z-7 nodded. "We've gone through every one of those buildings with a fine tooth comb, and I would be willing to stake my life that not a spot in any of them has been used as a headquarters by any agents of Montezuma!"

Jimmy frowned. "Then there must be some spot that I overlooked. Well, what about those two men you phoned me about who registered on this floor?"

Z-7 returned to his desk, picked up a folder. "They're in 1531, which is right next door to the suite in which Helen Powers and her daughter are confined. They seem to be Latin-Americans, and they have registered under the names of Gonzáles and Hernando. Their story is that the rooming house where they have been staying was visited by the explosive death this morning, and everybody in it annihilated, while they were out. Naturally, they say that they do not wish to return there. They told all this to one of our men who managed to get friendly with them in the barroom."

Jimmy Christopher tapped the edge of the chief's desk thoughtfully, while Tim Donovan watched him. "Have you checked on their story, Chief?"

Z-7 NODDED. "The lists of casualties for today mentions eight deaths at the boarding house they named. There is no flaw in their story—except for the fact that they wanted the fifteenth floor. They had a good reason for that, too. As you know, this is the top, and they feel they will have a little better chance of escaping alive in case of another visitation of the exploding death. They think that it may not reach so high up."

Jimmy Christopher laughed bitterly. "It reached me in an aeroplane. It reached hundreds of our aviators before the War Department could be induced to ground all flying units!"

Z-7 gazed into Jimmy Christopher's eyes for a long minute. Then he sighed, said: "I guess you're right, Operator 5. I—"

He stopped as a knock sounded at the door. A shirt-sleeved agent entered, reported tensely: "There's a report in from Gramercy Park, Chief! S-3 and P-12 are dead—blasted to pieces by the exploding death!"

Z-7 glanced at Jimmy Christopher with concern. "Two of our best men, Operator 5. You—know why they were posted there?"

Jimmy Christopher suddenly paled. "Chief! They were posted to guard Diane Elliot's house!" Jimmy gulped, addressed the shirt-sleeved agent. "You—you got a report on Miss Elliot? She's—safe?"

The agent shook his head. With reluctance he said slowly: "I'm sorry, Operator 5, Miss Elliot's apartment is empty. I sent two men down there at once. Neither Miss Elliot nor the Aztec princess whom she had in charge was in the apartment. They must have been kidnapped by Montezuma's men."

Jimmy Christopher whirled to Z-7. "You'll have to excuse me, Chief. I'm going down to Gramercy Park. Come on, Tim."

Z-7 made no move to restrain him. Jimmy Christopher and Tim were on their way out, when one of the phones on the chief's desk rang. "Wait!" said Z-7. "This may be—" He picked up the receiver, listened a moment, then said: "I'll have Operator 5 handle it. He's already been up against that set-up."

Jimmy looked inquiringly at the chief. Z-7 said: "Operator 5, I hate to ask you to do this—but you've got to pass up going to Gramercy Park. That was the agent posted in Room 1529, right next door to those two men who are registered here as Gonzáles and Hernando. We've got a dictograph planted in their room, and it seems that one of them is talking. If he's reporting to Aztec headquarters, it's our chance to check on locations. You're the logical one to take charge."

JIMMY CHRISTOPHER lowered his eyes to hide the intensity of feeling in them. For a moment he was silent, fighting a quiet battle to master his emotion. Then he said in a voice rendered thin by the effort he made to control it: "Okay, Tim. Take the car and go over there. Be careful, old-timer. And for God's sake, see if you can pick up Diane's trail."

He followed Z-7 and H-9 out into the corridor, and down past 1533, where Helen Powers and her mother were resting. Next door, in 1531, were the two men, Gonzáles and Hernando; and beyond them, in 1529, was posted the agent with the dictograph.

The agent looked up as they entered, removed the earphones from his head. "They've just finished talking," he reported, "most of it was inaudible, but I got a few words. Here they are." He handed to Jimmy Christopher a sheet of paper upon which he had taken a stenographic record of the conversation.

Jimmy read it without difficulty, translating: from Spanish into English as he went along:

"We should make our report, Hernando…. It is the hour at which our master will be waiting…." (second voice) "Master, we are ready… the girl and her mother are in the next…."

Jimmy glanced up from the sheet. "Chief! Those men in the next room are preparing to kidnap Helen Powers, right under our noses! They must have a carefully laid plan. They're probably getting instructions over the radio."

He stepped to the window, gazed out over the roofs of the city. "Their portable transmitter can't be very powerful. The Aztec headquarters is undoubtedly within the metropolitan area. Use direction finders—"

The chief dispatched an agent with terse instructions.

The agent at the dictograph suddenly raised his hand for silence. His lips formed the words: "They're talking again next door!"

Jimmy hastened to his side, watched the words take shape under the agent's pencil as he transcribed the Spanish conversation. Jimmy Christopher translated for the others as he read:

Come, Hernando, in ten minutes it will be time to strike. You will shoot out the lock of the connecting door, and we will break into the girl's room. The mother we may kill—but the girl must be brought unharmed to our Master....

The words droned off into silence, and Jimmy Christopher sprang into action. "Come on, Chief! They're going to break into 1533!"

H-8 produced a key from his pocket. "This'll open their door. I made sure to get it ready."

Jimmy Christopher took the key, hurried out into the corridor. He inserted the key in the lock of 1531, gave it a quick twist, and flung the door open. An automatic appeared in his hand as if by magic.

From within the room, at the instant that Jimmy had flung

the door open, came the sharp report of a gun. Two men, dark complexioned, sharp-featured, were standing close to the side door connecting with Room 1531, where Helen Powers was.

The shot had been fired by one of them into the lock, and the connecting door was now yawning open. Beyond it, Jimmy Christopher could see the startled faces of Helen Powers and her mother. But he had no time to call out to them. For the two dark-complexioned men turned on him, snarling, and raised their automatics....

JIMMY'S GUN barked twice, swiftly. The nearer of the two men pitched forward with a slug in his heart, while the second, who had just been about to step through the connecting door, was whirled around violently by the impact of Jimmy's bullet, and fell across the doorway into Room 1531. He groaned. Blood spurted from his side. He had been partly behind his companion, and Jimmy Christopher had to shoot him in the right side.

Operator 5 strode into the room, called through the connecting doorway: "It's all right, Mrs. Powers; you're safe!" He knelt beside the wounded man, demanded: "Talk quick! Where are your headquarters?"

The man groaned, glared up at Jimmy, twisted with pain, but made no answer. Jimmy tried again. "Your master will kill you for failing. Why not speak?"

The man's lips quivered, his lips clamped shut determinedly.

Z-7 had gone through the connecting door, and was quieting the two women. Jimmy Christopher pushed past H-9, stared about the room. On the bed was a suitcase, all packed and closed. Another suitcase lay on the floor. Jimmy stooped beside them, used his master keys, and in a moment had both suitcases open. One of them contained a complete radio set.

Operator 5 sprang to his feet, sped to the side of the wounded man. His eyes burned into the eyes of the other as he demanded: "Where is the message you just received over that radio?"

The other whispered feebly: "I—don't—know!"

Jimmy pursed his lips, thrust his hand into the man's pockets, one after the other. He found a notebook with the man's name in it, showing that he was Gonzalez. He found other odd trinkets, but no message.

He looked up to see that Z-7 was watching him from the doorway. Saying nothing, he turned to the body of the dead man, went through his pockets. This time he found what he had been looking for—a crumpled sheet of paper.

Jimmy hastily straightened out the paper. He motioned to H-9: "Take this down as I translate it!" And proceeded to read and translate:

All is ready. At six-fifteen promptly you will break through the connecting door and seize the girl, Helen Powers. Her mother you may kill if she resists; but the girl—at the peril of your lives, no harm must come to her!

At six-twenty-five exactly you will start to leave the hotel with the girl. Do not start a minute sooner, for at six-twenty-five exactly the explosive death will be sent into the street outside the hotel. This will distract the attention of the agents, and you will be able to leave by the back way. A car will await you, to conduct you and the girl to headquarters. Do not fail.

Do not harm the girl!

Slowly Operator 5 looked up from the perusal of that message. There was a calculating gleam in his eye. He was gazing speculatively through the open connecting doorway at Helen Powers....

Z-7 SAID urgently: "H-9! Have the street outside cleared of all people! It's six-twenty-three—you have two minutes to save anybody who may be out there. At six-twenty-five the explosive death will strike!"

H-9 hurried from the room to obey.

Operator 5 exclaimed: "Chief! This is our chance to discover where the Aztec headquarters are located!"

"How?" Z-7 asked, puzzled.

"Don't you see? There is to be a car waiting at the back entrance—to take Gonzalez and Hernando to their headquarters—with Miss Powers!"

"I still don't see—I'll have a radio report—"

"Wait, Chief!" Jimmy Christopher strode across the writhing body of the dying Gonzalez, into the next room. He seized both hands of Helen Powers.

"Miss Powers!" he said urgently. "You know that your father was killed by the agents of Montezuma; you know that the United States is threatened with slavery or complete annihilation!"

She stared at him wide-eyed. "Of course I do. Why?"

"Would you be willing to take a great risk—with me—to try to strike a blow to rid us of this menace—perhaps to avenge the death of your father?"

"I would!" she breathed. Her eyes shone, gray and deter-

A terrific explosion blossomed from the deck of the police-boat!

mined. "Even if it means my death! Whatever you say, I will do!" Her pretty, child-like face was suddenly transfigured with a shining zeal.

"Good!" he exclaimed. He left her, stepped across the threshold, and knelt beside the body of the dead Hernando. His swift, long fingers extracted from an inner pocket his flat makeup case. He set up the adjustable mirror on the floor, beside Hernando's body, laid out his tubes of pigment and plastic material.

Under the wondering gaze of Z-7, of Mrs. Powers, and of Helen Powers, his dexterous fingers began to stray swiftly over his own face, applying pigment here, molding plastic material there. From time to time he glanced at the dead Hernando. Soon his own keen, intelligent features had disappeared, to give place to those of the other.

So swiftly did he work, that at the end of four minutes he arose, after packing away his makeup case and mirror. Z-7 uttered a gasp of astonishment. "God!" he exclaimed. "Every time you do that I'm astounded. I'd swear you were a twin brother of that dead man!"

Helen Powers' eyes were shining. "You—you are going to take me with you to that car—instead of Hernando!"

Operator 5 nodded. "Exactly. As far as the Aztecs know, the plan to kidnap you has gone through. I will tie your hands, gag you, and take you out the back way. We will enter that car, and let them take us to their headquarters. I will say to them that my partner, Gonzalez, was killed in the escape."

Helen Powers said eagerly: "Let's do it. And may God grant us success!"

116

Operator 5 led her into the corridor. "We'll go down in the service elevator," he told Z-7. "Have a couple of your men appear to chase us, and fire at us—but be sure they shoot high! And don't forget, Chief, to have a couple of cars trail us!"

He shook hands quickly with his chief, and they left, the girl stumbling along with a gag in her mouth, her arms tied behind her, while Jimmy Christopher followed her, the living image of the dead Hernando....

CHAPTER 8
MACHINE GUN MESSAGE

WHEN JIMMY CHRISTOPHER had brought Helen Powers out of the Beacon and pushed her into the waiting sedan, he had not even bothered to look behind. He had been too busy appraising the Aztec agents.

Two men sat in front, and the car was in motion almost at once, roaring down the street with the throttle wide open. The man siding in front, next to the driver, said in Spanish to the one who sat in the rear beside Helen:

"Bring out the quick-firing gun, Léon. We will give them a doze of the exploding death!"

Jimmy Christopher glanced at him across the trembling form of Helen Powers. He was a gaunt man, with the hard face of a killer. Jimmy decided that he must be one of Montezuma's officers. Léon turned his bulging eyes on Helen Powers, and his glance traveled up and down her form admiringly. He switched to English:

117

"And you, pretty flower. You are very pretty, yes. But I do not understand why our master, the Emperor, wishes so badly to have you. For myself, I like the dark beauties of Mexico City." His eyes raised to Jimmy's. "Eh, Hernando? What say you?"

Jimmy Christopher shrugged. From where he sat, in the corner, he could not see out in back. He could still hear a few shots behind them, and knew that the Intelligence men were staging a good imitation of pursuit.

He glanced across at Léon. He must be careful now. Apparently, as Hernando, he was very well known to Léon. He could imitate the dead man's voice well enough, even though he had heard him speak only a few words. Anything he said might be the wrong thing, might arouse the suspicions of these men and destroy any chance of being taken by them to the Aztec headquarters. However, he could not remain silent all the time. He would have to talk sooner or later, and now was as good a time as any. So he shrugged at Léon's question, said carelessly in Spanish: "It is all one to me beauty or no beauty; as long as the emperor is pleased."

"Ha!" exclaimed Léon, his gaunt face twisting into a sardonic grin. "That is our Hernando—always the business! Tell me, Hernando, what has happened to Gonzalez?"

"Gonzalez," Jimmy told him, "was killed while we were escaping. The gringos fight well."

Léon clucked sympathetically. "Too bad!" He fondled the machine gun in his lap. "I think I will let off a few blasts at these fools who pursue us to avenge Gonzáles. What do you think, Hernando?"

"I think you had better not," Jimmy said hastily. "It may attract soldiers."

Léon laughed. "Soldiers! What do we care for soldiers! Soon we shall rule this whole country, and step on the necks of the proud Americans!"

Jimmy asked a question that he had been wanting an answer to, badly. "Is the Emperor Montezuma in New York now, Léon?"

"Did you not know?" Léon asked, surprised. "Ah, yes! I forget that you have been away from headquarters for almost a whole day. Our emperor has but just arrived from Mexico City by plane. It is from here that he will rule America. He brought with him two or three gringo prisoners. We are going to him now, with this pretty flower. He awaits us at the old Craigland estate, across the Hudson."

Jimmy Christopher's blood raced. His question was answered—better than he had expected. The Craigland estate—a massive old pile which stood like a fortress on the New Jersey side of the Hudson. Z-7 would spot it from his radio reports….

Important as that information was, Jimmy had just received equally as important information—the news that Montezuma was in New York—*with some prisoners!* Would one of them be John Christopher? Operator 5's blood raced with excitement. But he maintained an outward appearance of calm, asked: "The Princess Dolores has she been rescued from the Americans?"

"Of a surety, Hernando. We followed their car from the airport, the one in which that Operator 5 took her to the home of the newspaper girl. Soldiers wished to stop us at the Holland Tunnel, but we blasted them with this—" he tapped the machine gun affectionately—"and we rode past their riddled bodies. When he spotted the house of the newspaper girl, we made our plans just as we did here. Only a little while ago, another group of our men carried off the princess and the newspaper girl. They also are being brought to the Craigland estate. The emperor—"

Suddenly the driver turned, said in Spanish to Léon: "There is a black roadster behind us. It is coming too close, Léon. It has a more powerful motor than ours."

Léon swore, looked out through the rear window. Jimmy looked too, past Helen Powers' shoulder, and his blood went cold. He hadn't paid any attention to the pursuing cars, knowing that the agents had been instructed to keep far behind. But now he saw his own roadster, guessed that Tim was driving it. Tim must have come back to the hotel, he assumed, and taken up the chase. The boy, in his usual headstrong manner, was not counting the odds, but was bent on stopping the sedan.

Léon growled: "It is that same Operator 5. I recognize the car. He will soon be up to us!"

The driver threw over his shoulder in Spanish: "Give him a drink of your lead, Léon. He must not follow us to the river!"

Léon's thin lips twisted in a cold smile. "Now," he said softly, "I shall show you, Hernando, that I can use this plaything as well as you!"

He raised the sub-machine gun, and with the muzzle broke the rear window. Then he stuck it out, aimed at the tires of the pursuing roadster. He chuckled. "Watch him turn over when I puncture the tires!"

JIMMY CHRISTOPHER met the frightened gaze of

Helen Powers over her gag. And he acted.... He raised his left arm, with his hand opened stiffly; brought it around in a wide circle so that the edge of his hand caught Léon in a sharp blow at the base of the skull. It was a blow that seemed weak, ineffective to an observer not initiated in the art of jiu-jitsu. In reality, that particular spot at the base of the skull was one of the eighty nerve centers in the human body which, when struck at the proper angle, will paralyze the entire system. Jimmy Christopher knew all eighty of those nerve centers, as well as the proper way to strike at them. He had studied the "soft art" (which is a literal translation of the word, jiu-jitsu) under one of the most exacting teachers in the world—Kashawatska Hoia, the Imperial Instructor in Tokyo.

Léon, who had been facing toward the rear, suddenly let out his breath in a deep sigh as Jimmy's blow went home. Soundlessly he clumped, and his head lolled to one side. His body slipped from the seat to the floor at the feet of Helen Powers, and the machine gun dropped from his nerveless fingers.

So swift had been the flash of Jimmy Christopher's arm, that the two men in the front seat had not noticed it; neither had been looking back at the moment.

But now, the man next to the driver turned his head, exclaimed in Spanish: "Hold! Léon—!"

Jimmy interrupted: "He's been shot!" and snatched up the machine gun. He gave a good imitation of ferocity, saying: "The dog shot Léon through the broken window. I will make him pay!"

He swung the muzzle once more out of the window at the

swiftly nearing roadster, and pressed the trip. His slugs, aimed with precision, struck against the steel fender of the roadster in a peculiar rhythm.

As the two cars raced westward across the deserted city streets, the hail of lead from the sub-machine gun beat a strange tattoo on that fender—*dash, dash, dot, dot*—T.D.! T.D.!

THE CLEVER Irish lad in the roadster at once grasped the significance of the situation. Though he did not understand how Jimmy Christopher came to be in that sedan, he knew that only he could have sent that rapid-fire message drumming through the air against the steel fender, using the trip hammer of a machine gun for a sending key.

Jimmy Christopher held his breath while he watched the boy do marvelous tricks with the roadster, causing it to swerve from curb to curb without perceptibly diminishing its speed. Finally, at the Intersection of Eleventh Avenue, Tim jammed on the brakes, sent the roadster skidding in a wide, screeching curve, while the sedan roared west toward the river, free of pursuit. The Intelligence men in their cars had long since been outdistanced.

Jimmy turned from the rear window to hear the driver say: "That must be the finish of this Operator 5!"

Jimmy Christopher said nothing while the car slowed up at the riverfront. He could easily, now, have finished off the driver and the man beside him; but that was not his objective. He had to get into that house on the far side of the Hudson.

So, when the car pulled up along a wooden jetty, he got out, allowed himself and the girl, who was still bound and gagged, to be led toward a small power-boat moored alongside. Half a dozen men were waiting there, and each one of them seemed to have had his duties planned to the last detail for everything proceeded smoothly, and within two minutes, the boat was speeding with muffled motor across the Hudson.

The girl, cold and frightened now, huddled on a bench in the stern, with the sharp spray whipping into her face. Operator 5 stood beside her, and took advantage of the darkness to whisper a word of encouragement in her ear. "It's going off nicely, Miss Powers," he said. "We'll be inside that place in a few minutes. Intelligence knows where we're headed for, and we'll be able to count on some outside help." He reached and took off the gag from her mouth.

He stooped under cover of the darkness, and his swift fingers moved with uncanny certainty as he unfastened the cord that bound her wrists. He did not untie it entirely, but left it loose, so that she could drop it off if she had to. Then he took out his automatic, and pressed it into her cold hands.

"If you should need it later," he murmured.

He straightened just as a dark figure approached, walking spread-legged to balance himself against the rolling of the boat. Jimmy Christopher's eyes narrowed upon that figure—familiar even in the night: the heavy, brutish body, the coarse features as the man came nearer. It was Major Horgavo...!

His thick lips twisted in a smile, and he said to Jimmy: "You are the man named Hernando, are you not?"

Jimmy bowed, watching the other tensely. "I answer to that name, major," he said quietly.

Horgavo smiled his gross approval. "They tell me that you wrecked the car of Operator 5 with your machine gun fire."

Jimmy bowed again, murmured: "I am honored that my small action has been brought to your attention, major."

"Small action? Why, man, don't you realize that you destroyed the foremost Secret Service operator in our enemies ranks? There is a reward on that man's head—and you shall have it!"

"Thank you, sir."

"They tell me that you are an expert with the machine gun."

"I am quite familiar with it, sir."

"Then come. Follow me!" The major turned, gestured toward one of the men who were standing close by. "Watch the girl. Hernando is coming with me." Then he strode away along the tilting deck.

Jimmy followed him into the single low ceilinged cabin. There was no light here, for the boat was apparently riding without lights. The major stopped only a moment here, to pick up a sub-machine gun lying on the floor, and to hand it to Jimmy. He led the way out at once, took Jimmy's arm and guided him to the rail.

"Do you hear anything?" he asked.

Jimmy had already heard it. It was the low, muffled chug-chug of another powerboat coming down the river. He nodded, said: "Yes, major. I hear it. It is a boat—"

Horgavo bent close to him. "It is a river patrol. They, too, are riding without lights. In a moment they will cross our path. It will be your duty to spray their deck with the machine gun. Do you understand?"

Jimmy said: "Yes, sir. I understand."

The jaw muscles of Jimmy Christopher's face bulged as he fingered the tommy-gun. He hoped that the patrol would pass them in the dark.

THE SOUND of the police motor grew louder, and Jimmy, glancing up and down the deck, saw that he was not the only one with a machine gun. A half dozen forms were lined up along the rail, waiting tensely. The moment they were challenged they would unleash a vicious hail of lead that would mow down every living man on the deck of the patrol.

Horgavo remained beside him, staring into the night, and Operator 5 hoped fervently that the police boat would miss them. Nothing must interfere now with his gaining entrance to that gloomy building high on the cliffs.

And just then they were discovered. Across the water they heard a low-voiced order; a burst of brilliant light came into being, and a huge spotlight centered upon their boat. At the same time, Horgavo shouted a hoarse order: "Lights! Fire!"

From the rail on both sides of Jimmy Christopher a hail of vicious lead tore from a half dozen machine guns in the direction of the police boat, while from the roof of the cabin their own searchlight clicked on to flood the patrol with light.

Only for a moment did those two spotlights remain on, then they were shattered by the rapid—fire slugs now coming from both boats. Now, auxiliary searchlights, fore and aft of the police boat began to glower, throwing a dull beam across the water.

A storm of lead tore across the deck of the Aztec boat, and cries of agony sounded as men fell. Horgavo, standing beside

Jimmy, exclaimed hoarsely: "It is the armored power-boat. We cannot fight them! I must signal the Master!" He turned, ran in the direction of the cabin, and reappeared in a moment with a Very pistol which he raised in the air and fired.

Two green balls of fire described a graceful parabola in the air from the muzzle of the gun. At the same time, the barrage from the patrol-boat ceased, and a voice called out to them: "Cut out your engine till we pull alongside, or we'll rake you again. You're under arrest!"

And then, as if in answer to the Very pistol's signal, a tremendous searchlight fingered down upon the river from the Craigland house on the cliffs. It swept across the deck of Horgavo's boat, revealing the still bodies lying in pools of blood. That volley from the police boat had done plenty of damage. The searchlight kept moving, played upon the police patrol, and remained there. From across the intervening gap between the two boats Jimmy Christopher heard a voice order: "Full speed ahead. Get out of that light!"

Too well did Jimmy know what would follow. And it did. Suddenly, as if the thing had occurred spontaneously, a terrific explosion sounded from the deck of the police boat. The screams of men echoed above the sound of the detonation, and the air was suddenly filled with cascading fragments of torn and battered bodies. Then quiet descended upon the river once more.

The police boat raced madly, aimlessly across the water, with its throttle wide open. No hand was guiding the tiller. It was a boat filled with the torn shreds of what had just been brave men. For a moment, the spotlight followed that boat in its erratic course, then it suddenly clicked off, and darkness hid the gory bits of floating jetsam that littered the surface of the river. The exploding death had come and gone....

Jimmy Christopher's thoughts were bitter as the boat nosed its way into a dark shed at the foot of the tall rock far below the Craigland house....

CHAPTER 9
THE MAN WHO KILLED
OPERATOR 5

THE DECK of the power-boat was a shambles. The boards were slippery with blood. They had started out from the New York side with eight men; now, only two besides Horgavo and Operator 5 were left on their feet. The barrage from the police boat had accounted for the others.

Horgavo ordered the two men to take care of the casualties. Then he motioned to Jimmy Christopher. "Come, Hernando. We will bring the lady up to the emperor!"

Jimmy Christopher felt the girl shiver under his grasp. She turned frightened eyes to him, was about to blurt out something. But he squeezed her arm. "Steady, Miss Powers," he whispered. "You've gone this far—go through with it."

At last, they reached the top of the cliff, came out into a wide clearing. The big house loomed dark and ugly, with one side of it sitting at the very edge of the rock, overlooking the river.

Dark shapes moved everywhere, with small flashlights. Jimmy discerned many cars grouped in the clearing, and he noted, as

127

they followed Horgavo toward the wide, unlit entrance of the house, that the license plates on those cars were representative of many states. They were from Pennsylvania, Jersey, Massachusetts, Connecticut. Montezuma's agents, apparently, were assembling from all over the country.

They entered through two huge doors of solid oak, and stood in a brightly lit, low-ceilinged foyer. Jimmy saw why no light had shown out while they were climbing the path down below—all the windows were tightly shuttered. Men in uniforms were hurrying to and fro here. All who passed close saluted Horgavo, and some of them nodded in recognition to Jimmy. He assumed that as Hernando he must be known to them, and nodded in response.

Horgavo bowed to Helen Powers, said: "If you will come with me now, I will present you to my master. He has been unhappy ever since you—er—left him in Mexico City. You, fair lady, are one of the principal reasons for transferring our headquarters to this place."

He took her unwilling arm, and threw over his shoulder to Jimmy Christopher: "Wait for me in the officer's room, Hernando. I have more work for you tonight."

Jimmy saluted, watched Helen Powers go unwillingly with the major. Then he turned to inspect his surroundings. The other two men who had come up the path with them had already left, and he was alone to do as he pleased.

He noted that many of the officers were turning to the left down a broad corridor, and he followed them. He turned a bend in the hallway, and saw that these men were all going into one of the rooms off the corridor.

He strolled up past the open doorway, and peered into the room. There must have been at least a hundred men in there, all standing about in attitudes of expectancy.

Over their heads, at the far end, Operator 5 saw that a makeshift altar had been erected, over which brooded the vicious, stone carved features of the obscene god, Huitzilopochtli.

Jimmy Christopher's blood raced as he thought that if the Aztecs mastered the country, altars to this deity might be set up throughout the land. He turned away from the scene in revulsion, stopped short at sight of the small procession that was approaching from the other end of the corridor.

About a dozen officers in brilliant uniform, with swords clanking at their sides, were marching in escort to the Princess Dolores.

All the men in the hall stood at attention as she passed, and saluted. Horgavo's eyes lighted on Jimmy, and he bent, whispered in her ear. The dark gaze of Dolores settled upon Operator 5, and he stiffened, saluted as he had seen the others do. Dolores' full red lips parted in a smile, and she raised her hand, motioned him to come closer.

JIMMY STEPPED up near her. His heart was beating fast. He had taken the precaution this time, to cover that birthmark on the back of his hand, by spreading a tinted wax over it. But Dolores was a woman, and it is more difficult to deceive a woman than a man. She had looked into his eyes once before, and he could not avoid her gaze now.

But there was no hint of recognition in her voice as she said to him: "Major Horgavo tells me that you are the man who brought about the death of Operator 5."

Jimmy bowed, lowering his eyes.

The princess sighed. "He was a brave man. I would have preferred to have had him captured alive. I would have given much to watch him upon the torture rack!"

She spoke in Spanish, and Jimmy Christopher answered in the same language. "I am sorry, your highness, that I did not know. I would have saved him for you." The princess' eyes became dreamy. She said musingly to Horgavo:

"Do you know, major, that this Operator 5 was the only man who ever aroused my interest? There was something dynamic about him—a certain poised strength that made me want to conquer him. I never thought that a man like Operator 5 would meet his death in a minor chase, from machine-gun bullets!"

Jimmy Christopher watched Horgavo's sultry eyes play upon the supple form of the princess. It could be readily seen that his desire for her was so strong that it bid fair to overcome his discretion. "It shall be my endeavor, your highness," he said gallantly, "to make you forget that—that spy!" He spat the last word out venomously. He was deathly jealous of a man whom he believed to be dead.

The princess shrugged, resumed her stately walk toward the room with the altar. She threw over her shoulder negligently at Jimmy: "You may come with us, and view the sacrifices—"

Jimmy Christopher was about to bow and ask to be excused, for he wanted to be free to explore the house. But he froze into silence at the next words of the princess: "I shall, at least, derive some satisfaction from watching the death agonies of this woman whom Operator 5 is supposed to have loved. She will be the first on the altar." And she added savagely, gloatingly: "We will see if this much vaunted hero can come back from the grave to save her!"

Automatically, as in a daze, Jimmy fell in behind the princess's retinue. Diane to be sacrificed on the altar! To have her heart torn from her still-living body as he had seen done in Mexico City—to have her still living, palpitating heart offered up to Huitzilopochtli in the bloody hands of those barbarous priests!

Operator 5 was but a number in the archives of the United States Intelligence. Yet he was human.

His eyes had become a dull, murky blue; his jaw muscles were bunched into hard ridges as he tried to keep from throwing himself upon Dolores and choking the life from her.

As soon as they were within the room, the doors were closed. Jimmy was puzzled at this, for he had expected that the Emperor Montezuma would himself preside at such a sacrifice He had the explanation in a moment when he heard the princess say to Horgavo, with a scornful curve of her lips: "My father is so infatuated with that American girl whom you brought, that he cannot even spare the time for the sacrifices! He should be careful; I saw that girl's eyes, and she hates him!" The princess shrugged. "If the girl kills him in his sleep some night, I shall not be too surprised."

Horgavo smiled, said very low, so that none could hear except Operator 5; who was close behind them: "If that should happen, your highness would become the Empress of the Aztecs. And you would have no more loyal servant than—myself!"

The princess made no reply, but turned her eyes to the altar, where two white-robed priests had appeared. The officers in the room had divided to form a lane down which the princess and her retinue could approach the altar, and Jimmy Christopher had followed close behind.

NOW HE watched as the two priests prostrated themselves before the stone idol, then arose to their knees and began to recite strange incantations. A hush fell upon the entire room. The droning voices of the priests rose higher and higher until they reached a screaming pitch of frenzy. Finally one of them seized a long, gleaming knife, and whirled it above his head three times, touched its point to his own forearm, drawing blood.

He lowered his eyes, pointed a scrawny finger at Dolores. "O Princess!" he intoned, as if speaking a ritual, "Do you bring an offering to the great God, Huitzilopochtli? Do you wish power and glory? Do you wish to know the secrets of life and death and love and hate? Then bring to the altar an offering of a live thing, and Huitzilopochtli will speak!"

The priest Mazatlan, lowered the knife, continued to stare at the princess.

Dolores spoke slowly, clearly, so that all in the room could hear: "Mazatlan, High Priest of the temple of Huitzilopochtli!" she intoned. "I bring two offerings. One is the heart of a young girl, the other is the heart of an old man. But both will be welcome to Huitzilopochtli; for they are the hearts of those who were loved by a bitter foe of the Aztec Empire. Let them die, and then I will ask my questions of Huitzilopochtli!"

She turned to Horgavo, ordered: "Bring in the girl, Diane Elliot."

Almost at once the door opened. Diane Elliot appeared there. Her face was pale, but she held her chin high. She was attired in a long white robe that fell to her feet, with a girdle at the waist. Her hands were tied behind her back.

Behind her, with one huge paw on her shoulder appeared a giant of a mestizo, whose coarse, brutish features were twisted into a leer of expectancy. This must be her jailer.

Diane stopped a moment in the doorway, and her hopeless eyes darted around the room as if in search of someone. When she saw the roomful of men, the two priests, the darkly arrogant princess, she seemed to shrink back. But the mestizo pushed her forward roughly, and she stumbled toward the altar under the fanatical gaze of all in the room.

She recovered her balance with difficulty, and stood facing the princess, who said to her acridly: "Before you are sacrificed to Huitzilopochtli, pale one, I will give you some news. Your gallant knight, Operator 5, has been killed—killed, do you hear? There is none to help you here. We shall see if you can die as bravely as he would have died!"

Diane Elliot staggered under the news. Her breasts heaved with emotion. Jimmy, watching her, wanted to cry out to her, to tell her that it was not the truth. But he waited.

Diane, by a supreme effort, mastered her emotion. She swallowed hard, said in a low voice: "I am ready—to die, too!"

ONE OF the priests stepped close to her, seized her by both elbows from behind, and forced her down on her back upon the great stone set at the foot of the image. Mazatlan, the high priest, still held the long, curved knife in his scrawny hand. Now he approached, gazing down upon her with his gaunt face as obscene in its blood thirsty fanaticism as that of the bestial god he served.

He raised the knife high, spoke in Spanish, in a high-pitched, screaming voice: "Huitzilopochtli! Great god of the Aztecs! In return for this offering, bring us victory! Bring strength and greatness to Emperor Montezuma, and to the Princess Dolores! Make our people the rulers of the earth!"

And he reached down one long-fingered, claw-like hand, gripped the blouse of Diane's robe, and tore it open. Diane uttered a shriek, but she was hapless in the grip of the second priest.

She shut her eyes as the sharp blade described a flashing arc in the air, descended toward her white body.

Until then, Jimmy Christopher had stood tense, waiting. He had not dared to act until the lustful attention of everyone in the room was riveted upon the altar. Now he moved.

He no longer had his own gun, for he had given it to Helen Powers. He took a quick step to the left, which brought him alongside Horgavo. His left hand reached into Horgavo's holster, while his right, bunched into a hard-knuckled fist, came up in a smashing blow to the side of the major's chin.

The blow sent Horgavo crashing backward to the floor, and Jimmy's hand came away with his automatic. Suddenly the room was in pandemonium. Men shouted, scrambled toward Jimmy. The Princess Dolores turned a livid face toward his face momentarily robbed of all its beauty by the rage that twisted her features. She screamed something unintelligible at him— something that was unintelligible because it was drowned by two quick reports from the automatic that had sprung up like a live thing in Jimmy Christopher's hand.

The two priests were thrown backward by the impact of the slugs, and their bodies went hurtling into the stone image of Huitzilopochtli, then slumped to the floor of the altar. They were both dead before their bodies came to rest on the cold stone. The knife went slithering from the grasp of the executioner, lay almost at Diane's feet.

In the second of astounded silence that followed those two shots, Operator 5 launched himself like a rocket through the throng about the altar, bounded up its steps at a single leap. His movements were swift, well-coördinated; he had shot with his left hand, with which he was equally as accurate as with the right. Now he snatched up the long knife, stepped to the side of the bound girl, and pushed her roughly over. With a single slash he cut the cords that held her wrists, saying as did so: "It's I, Diane! Jimmy!"

Diane Elliot's glad cry rang through the room. "Jimmy! Thank God!"

Operator 5 lifted her swiftly, pushed her toward the edge of the altar. Men were swarming toward them now, guns flashed the room.

Now he thrust Diane behind him, turned to meet the rush

of uniformed men who swarmed about them. Several guns exploded, harmlessly; for the fighting was at too close quarters. Jimmy clubbed his automatic in his right fist, and his arms pistoned in and out.

He threw over his shoulder: "Diane! The door! Get it open!" His fists kept flailing at the attacking officers; each blow that he struck was carefully placed, directed at a vital spot. He stood there, fighting coolly, methodically, taking advantage of the lack of elbow room of his opponents. He was a cold, dangerous fighting machine. His face was set, expressionless, but his blue eyes darted everywhere, seemed to see everything. Pistol butts were raised against him, swords flashed; but hardly a blow reached him.

AND WHILE he fought coolly, calculatingly, the eyes of one woman were on him with dawning wonder and amazement. The Princess Dolores watched him, with her red lips slightly parted, her breast rising and falling with each blow he struck. She was like some old Roman empress watching a barbarian gladiator fight in the arena for his life. Never had she seen such an exhibition of cold fighting nerve.

Suddenly the voice of Major Horgavo rose above the noise of the fighting. He had gotten to his feet from the floor, his jaw blue and swollen. He had snatched a revolver from the hand of one of the officers on the fringe of the attackers, and now he shouted:

"Stand back, all of you." He sprang up on the altar, from where he had an unobstructed view of Jimmy and Diane, over the heads of the fighting men.

At his command the officers fell back, leaving several of their number on the floor. The major lowered his gun to cover Jimmy Christopher, and at the same time Diane cried out: "Jimmy. Come. The door is open!"

Her voice was drowned by the roar of the major's revolver; but the bullet went high—for the Princess Dolores had sprung up on the altar after him, and just as he pulled the trigger, she had knocked up his gun hand. "I want that man alive!" she exclaimed.

Jimmy had whirled at Diane's call. Now he lunged through the open doorway after her, just as the other officers surged forward at the Princess's command. And Jimmy slammed the door in their faces!

He glanced around at the room they were in. It was small, dark, lit by only a single, small, electric bulb. It was the pen in which the prospective sacrificial victims were confined. And there was one other victim there—John Christopher!

Another huge mestizo, like the one who had brought in Diane, stood guard beside him, with an automatic in his hand. Before the mestizo could bring his weapon up, Jimmy Christopher stepped in, brought up the edge of his open hand in a short, cutting blow that landed at a point about two thirds of an inch below the mestizo's eye.

Though Jimmy had seemed only to hit him lightly, the mestizo uttered a shriek of agony, dropped the gun, and raised both hands to his face. That blow had paralyzed his optic nerves. He would be unable to see for hours. He doubled over in agony, uttering screen after scream.

And though Jimmy's face was distorted into the features of

another man—though he was skillfully disguised—John Christopher exclaimed gladly: "Jimmy!"

The door behind them urged open under the influx of attackers from the other room, and Jimmy swung quickly, snapped a shot at the face that appeared in the opening. The face disappeared in a spray of blood, and Jimmy, moving with swift precision, drew a knife from his pocket. The blade snapped open at his touch on a hidden spring, and he slashed twice at his father's bonds.

John Christopher's hands came free. The two men, father and son, wasted no time in explanations. All that John Christopher needed to know was that this was Jimmy, and that Jimmy had come out of the next room fighting.

With a single step John Christopher reached the side of the screaming mestizo, stooped and picked up the revolver he had dropped. Then they each took one of Diane's arms, hurried her toward the door in the opposite wall.

The other door was coming open again; it swung wide, and the doorway was jammed with uniformed officers eager to be the first through. They got in their own way in the narrower entrance, and Jimmy turned his automatic on them, kept the trigger down while it sprayed lead into the thick of them.

Then he turned, and with lead whining wildly into the small room from the sacrificial chamber, he darted out after Diane and his father, kicked the door closed behind him.

They found themselves in a narrow, unlighted passageway. John Christopher threw back: "Follow me! I know the way here."

No unnecessary words were spoken. These two fighting men

had been in ticklish spots together before. They could almost read each other's minds in a crisis. And Diane was too overcome yet with emotion at finding Jimmy alive again—at the sudden escape from the sacrificial altar—to be able to say anything. She was content to go where they took her, to be guided by them. Now with peril all about them, she felt unaccountably safe…!

CHAPTER 10
THE CHALLENGE

THE PASSAGEWAY into which John Christopher had led Diane and Jimmy was unlighted. It had no windows. The floor creaked under them. John Christopher called back to Jimmy: "I know just where this goes, son. I was brought along here to the sacrifice room. If we can get down to the end, there's a door with only a single guard, then a short stairway that takes you out through a rear entrance. If we can make it—"

Jimmy Christopher could hear Diane's quick breathing just in front of him, and he pressed her arm reassuringly. "You two go on ahead. I'll hold them here. And when you get out, find Z-7; I'm sure he's out here by now, preparing to attack. Tell him to wait till I give the signal, or all his men will be wiped out by the exploding death!"

John Christopher demanded suspiciously: "What do you plan to do, lad? If it's a question of holding them a while, to give Diane a chance to get out, I'm the man to do it. I'm old. I've nothing much to live for—"

"Trust me, dad!" Jimmy whispered urgently. "I'm not sacrificing my life uselessly, I promise you that. I've got to cripple that mysterious exploding death. Now go!"

He heard his father say huskily: "All right, Jimmy. Come, Diane!"

Operator 5 heard them move down the passageway, but did not turn. He was facing the door now, and he dropped to one knee. From the lining of his coat, he extracted a long, pencil-like tube. It was made of dull metal, and there was a cap at one end, with a smell pin sticking out of it. He had this in his right hand, his eyes intently fixed on that door. In the darkness he could just discern the dark shape of the officer he had shot, lying inert on the floor.

Jimmy swiftly raised the tube in his hand, and drew out the pin. Then he held it poised, while the watch on his wrist ticked off three seconds. From where he knelt he could hear the click of a machine gun bolt through the door, and he waited no longer. He drew back his arm, hurled the tube straight at the door.

This tube was a modification of the Mills bomb, used extensively by the police of large cities. But unlike the Mills bomb, its area of damage was confined to a radius of only four feet. He had developed this pencil bomb in his laboratory at Address Y, and had perfected it only after tireless experiments with varying quantities of explosive, and with various containers. This was the first time since he had perfected it that he had occasion to use it.

Even as he threw it, he dropped prone on the ground, placed fingers in both his ears. He waited there in the darkness for what seemed an eternity; but it was only two seconds—hardly enough for the machine gunner on the other side to get his weapon in position. And then suddenly, a deafening explosion shook the walls and floor of the passageway....

THE TERRIFIC force of that concentrated detonation jarred Operator 5 even where he lay, a dozen feet from the door. The sound of tinkling, broken glass and of rending, cracking wood followed the explosion. He took his fingers from his ears, raised his head, then got to his feet.

A dark, gaping hole showed where the door had been. Groans and screams of wounded men came to him. The lights in the room beyond the doorway had all been shattered by the concussion, and he could distinguish a milling, panicky crowd of figures there. Between him and them, at the spot where the pencil bomb had exploded, there was a wide gap in the floor.

Jimmy Christopher turned silently and made his way in the opposite direction along the passageway after his father and Diane. They were not in the corridor. He hoped they had had time to get outside the mansion.

Behind him now, over the agonized groans of dying men, he heard the voice of the Princess Dolores: "Fools! Why do you wait here! That passageway leads to the cliff entrance. Go around and head them off!"

Jimmy hurried on, groping ahead of him for the end of the passageway. And then he heard Horgavo's smooth voice, saying: "Let us try them with the exploding death, your highness. This Operator 5 had already killed some of our best men. Why send more men against him, when we can destroy him in a moment?"

"All right, Horgavo," the princess assented. "Order them to direct the exploding death to cover the cliffs behind the house!"

141

Jimmy's blood ran cold. He had seen the terrible results of the exploding death. His father and Diane must even now be coming out of the mansion. He shuddered at the thought of what would happen to them.

And as if in answer to that very thought of his came the words of the princess once more: "They will all three be shattered into bits. I am sorry that I cannot capture that Operator 5 alive. I would let the other two go if I could make that man my prisoner!"

And Jimmy Christopher suddenly, without thinking, called out from the darkness of the passageway in Spanish: "You have your wish, princess! I am still here. Let my father and the girl go out unharmed, and I will give myself up!"

Abruptly, at the sound of his words, there was a hush in the small room at the end of the passageway. Even the men who were groaning with pain ceased their laments for a moment.

The princess exclaimed: "It is he! Bring a flashlight!"

Someone clicked on a flashlight, but Jimmy Christopher's automatic slid out of his holster, and it barked once. The flashlight was shattered, and the man who held it uttered a yelp of pain.

Jimmy called out coldly: "Countermand the order you just gave for the exploding death, princess, and I will give myself up. Then you can turn on your flashlights."

The princess raised her voice: "Do you give me your word that you will surrender?"

"I give it!" Operator 5 said simply.

The princess ordered Horgavo: "Call back the one who went with my order. At once!"

Horgavo grumbled, but he obeyed. Jimmy, listening attentively, heard him shout out to someone to return.

Jimmy Christopher stood erect, squared his shoulders, and walked slowly toward the shambles created by his pencil bomb. A dozen rays of light from as many torches were concentrated on him, almost blinding him. Someone called out from the other room: "Wait! There is a hole in the floor."

He stood still, while boards were brought, placed over the gaping hole in the floor, so that he could cross. He stepped across into the room, and almost slipped on the blood of the men who had been killed by the pencil bomb.

The cold voice of the Princess Dolores ordered: "Seize him!" ROUGH HANDS gripped his arms, twisted them behind his back. He was held helpless while the princess stepped close, took a flashlight from one of the men, and held it close to his face, shining straight into his eyes.

"Operator 5," she said, "you are a fool. You deliberately sacrificed yourself for a girl and a man. It is the weakness that will destroy all of you Americans—your senseless gallantry."

Jimmy said nothing, but stared into the eye of the flashlight. His lips were set grimly. The princess was right. He had given himself into her cruel hands to save Diane and his father.

He said coolly: "Thank you for your compliment, princess. But it is not gallantry that will destroy us. It is the mysterious force which your father controls."

Dolores' cold laugh tinkled like ice in a glass. "It is too bad that the leaders of your country do not understand that as well as you do, Operator 5. They are hard to convince. But the lesson we will give them tonight is one that they will never forget. There are soldiers climbing the cliff outside now—thousands of them. And in one hour, they will all be destroyed. No doubt your father and that girl will be with them—so that your sacrifice is in vain, you see."

She was laughing at him. "And now, Operator 5, I shall give myself the pleasure of seeing you on the torture rack," She swung to Horgavo. "Take him away, and prepare him! We shall have some sport for the next hour!"

Jimmy Christopher allowed himself to be led away by Horgavo and two other men. The last sound in his ears was the cold laughter of the princess.

THEY TOOK him back through the sacrificial chamber, where the bodies of the two dead priests lay in a water of their own blood; then out into the broad hallway, where men stared at him curiously.

They led Jimmy Christopher down a flight of stairs, and past an open door. A peculiar, humming sound came from that room, and Horgavo motioned for Jimmy's two captors to stop a moment, then stepped inside.

Jimmy glanced after him, saw that the hum came from a tremendous generator that was set in the concrete floor, and rose through an opening in the ceiling into the room above. Machinery was arranged in orderly fashion along the two opposite walls of this room—huge, black steel monsters over which men in greasy overalls were climbing, oiling and testing them.

Jimmy's keen eyes traveled over the various items, classifying them in his mind. He turned quickly to the man at his left, said in Spanish: "Those are the instruments by which you spread the exploding death, are they not?"

The man grinned, nodded. "From that room, Señor Operator 5, the exploding death goes out all over your country. Soon it will be set in motion again—but you will not be interested. You will be screaming in agony while the Princess Dolores watches and laughs!"

Jimmy swung his eyes back into the room. Horgavo was talking to a bald-headed, sharp-eyed man in white smocks who was nodding and smiling. Jimmy heard this man say in English:

"All is ready, major. The rarefying element is in position, set to saturate the area from here down to the river. At the word, everything on the cliffs below will explode. Not a single one of the soldiers will be left alive!"

He motioned toward the one wall against which no machinery was erected.

On this wall was an immense map of the United States in detail. The reading matter on this map was so fine that it could not be read with the naked eye, but a huge magnifying glass hung on a projecting steel elbow in front of the map; and the particular spot before which it was suspended stood out in bold relief, magnified fifty times.

A BEAM of light, emanating from a lens in one of the machines on the opposite wall was lancing across the room, and was focused on the map through the magnifying glass. Jimmy Christopher immediately recognized the spot on the map as corresponding to the place on the edge of the water where he had landed with Horgavo and Helen Powers. It was there that the forces of Z-7 were concentrating now, awaiting a signal from him. And it was there that the exploding death was focused to strike!

Horgavo was saying: "That is well, Doctor Maltbie. If they should begin the attack before the hour, you will be notified."

He left the white-smocked man, came out into the corridor, smirking at Jimmy. "Now you have seen the device that has struck death to your countrymen, Operator 5. Do you understand it?"

Jimmy Christopher nodded. "I understand the principle, Horgavo," he said quietly. He nodded his head toward the white-smocked man who was moving about in the other room. "I also know that renegade scientist. Maltbie is the inventor of an electronic ray that decomposes the atmosphere at any given spot with the speed of lightning. It is that ray which he is generating in there."

Horgavo stared, surprised. "You are clever, Operator 5!"

Jimmy Christopher went on, stating the swift confusions he had readied, and waiting for Horgavo to confirm them.

"The electronic ray is discharged by means of that vacuum"— he nodded toward a huge round, duralumin-enclosed piece of machinery at which the white-smocked scientist was bending—"and travels with the speed of light toward the spot at which it is projected. At that spot, it rarefies the atmosphere so suddenly that all pressure from the outside is removed from any object in the area, and the object explodes due to the pressure from within. Is that right, Horgavo?"

Maltbie, the scientist, had heard what Jimmy said. Now he turned, and his small, bird-like eyes settled on Operator 5. He came out of the room, still staring at Jimmy. He muttered: "There was only one other man in the world who knew the secret!"

Jimmy relaxed in the grip of his two captors, said bitingly: "That man was George Powers, Maltbie! But unlike you, Powers died in an effort to save his country. You"—his words bit like acid at the scientist—"have sold your soul to the devil! You have betrayed your country, Maltbie!"

The scientist shrank from the hot rage in Jimmy's eyes, turned and slunk back into the room. Horgavo said shortly: "Come!" and the two men dragged Jimmy along after him.

The major led the way to the end of the corridor, thrust open an iron-grilled door. Jimmy was pushed roughly in, and the two men and Horgavo came in after him. They were in a small, cell-like room, absolutely bare of furniture. The two men each seized one of Jimmy's wrists, stretched his arms out on either side of him, and snapped handcuffs on them. Then they clicked the free end of each pair of handcuffs to a ring set in the wall, so that Jimmy stood spread-eagled against the wall, facing the iron-barred door.

Horgavo watched, smiling with smug satisfaction. Then, when Jimmy seemed helpless, he stepped closer, and with his finger nails he raked the make-up from Jimmy's face. He said, "It is not fitting that you should meet your death with the features of one of our own men."

He kept on raking Jimmy's face until none of the make-up remained. His inquisitive fingers removed the small plates from Jimmy's nostrils, and he examined them carefully nodding in appreciation. "You are a very clever man, Operator 5," he said. "Too clever to live!"

His hands rapidly went through Jimmy's pockets, removing article after article. He examined them all with growing amazement as he realized their possible use. He handed each article to one of the other men as he finished with it.

While this was going on, Jimmy tentatively tried the handcuffs that stretched his arms taut on either side of him. And his blood chilled. Those cuffs were not the usual kind. Ordinarily he could so manipulate his wrists as to release himself from a set of handcuffs within a few minutes. But he knew at once that it would be impossible in this case. These cuffs closed tighter than any he had ever seen, and they had been clamped high on his wrist, just above the ulna. Even if he were able to come free of them, it would take hours of painful manipulation. And there was less than an hour to spare before Z-7's men were to be annihilated down there on the cliffside—with John Christopher and Diane among them, no doubt.

JIMMY'S PLAN of action had been essentially simple—relying on that very simplicity for success. He had expected to be left alone for long enough to effect his release, and then, with the knowledge of the exact location of the exploding death device, first to find Montezuma and kill him, and then to wreck that device.

Now, however, Jimmy Christopher realized that his plan

would not work. These men had done their job only too well; he could not get free of those handcuffs. Like the good strategist that he was, he did not stick to a worthless plan until it was futile.

At once he began to work on a new one. He had not been blind to the ardent glances that Major Horgavo had cast in the direction of the Princess Dolores; neither had he been blind to the fact that Horgavo was deathly jealous of himself. This was a weakness of the enemy, and like a good general, he used it.

He said dryly: "I suppose you will be quite relieved to see me die, major?"

Horgavo laughed, showing his large, white teeth. "It will be a pleasure which I could never think of denying myself, Operator 5."

Jimmy made sure he spoke loud enough for the other two men in the cell to hear. "It is too bad, major," he drawled, "that you have to win in such a cowardly fashion!"

Horgavo's cheek flushed. Involuntarily he raised his open hand, brought it sharply across Christopher's face in a vicious slap that left a livid mark. "You call me a coward!"

Jimmy's cheek smarted from the blow, but he managed to grin under it. His hands were manacled to the wall, but his legs were free. With his right foot he lashed out vigorously, and the toe of his shoe caught Horgavo in the left shin.

With a howl of agony the major doubled over, dancing about on one foot, while the other two officers gazed in dismay. Jimmy said to the groaning major: "If the princess were to see you now, what would she think of you? There are tears in your eyes!"

Horgavo straightened, and white hate shone from his eyes.

His gross mouth twisted into a merciless leer. "When I am through with you," he snarled, "the princess will find no pleasure in looking at you!"

He raised his automatic, brought it down in a raking blow that tore a long furrow in Jimmy's left cheek, bared it to the bone.

Operator 5 tensed, said deliberately:

"You are brave, major—while I'm handcuffed to the wall. Would you be so brave if we faced each other with weapons?"

Horgavo sneered. "Go on. Talk. You will be whining soon!"

He transferred the automatic from his right hand to his left, prepared to rake it across Jimmy's other cheek. But from the doorway an imperious feminine voice called out sharply: "Stop!"

The eyes of Horgavo and the other two men swiveled toward the doorway, and they stood stiffly at attention, saluting. For there stood the regally beautiful Dolores. Her face was cold, expressionless, but her bosom was heaving. She stepped into the cell, stared at Horgavo. "Why do you strike this man? Were you not ordered to prepare him for the torture? Am I to be cheated of the pleasure of witnessing this man's agony?"

Horgavo stammered: "He insulted me, your highness. I lost my temper."

She laughed coldly. "Fool! Can you not see that he is deliberately trying to goad you into killing him? He has no taste for the things that my father and I will order done to him!"

Jimmy said tauntingly: "If you feel yourself insulted, major, why don't you demand satisfaction? I'll be glad to fight you with any weapons you name!"

Horgavo sputtered with rage, but dared not strike again....

THE PRINCESS eyed Jimmy speculatively for a while, her gaze resting on the bleeding furrow in his cheek. "You are a brave man, Operator 5," she said. "Also, you are a fool!" She motioned to Horgavo and the two others. "Leave us. I wish to talk to this man alone!"

Horgavo started to protest, but his words froze at the glance she gave him. Silently the three officers filed out of the cell. The princess waited, tapping her foot impatiently, until they were alone. Then she stepped close to Jimmy, her eyes flashing, her breasts heaving excitedly.

She drew herself up to her full height before him. "Look at me, Operator 5," she commanded. "Am I not beautiful?"

Jimmy gazed at her appreciatively. "You are very beautiful, princess!"

Suddenly her eyes flashed. "You are a fool to waste your loyalty on a lost cause. America is doomed!"

Jimmy Christopher said nothing. His lips were set tight, and his blue eyes met her dark ones in an uncompromising gaze.

She went on, the words rushing from her lips. "But you are so brave, so clever, so strong! You face death and torture so nonchalantly!" Her lips were close to his now as she whispered: "I could have you tortured—tortured until you scream from sheer agony which no man can endure. Our priests know refined tortures which can keep you gasping in pain for days and days, praying for death to relieve you. Operator 5, I could make you plead with me for death. But I offer you life!"

She paused, and Jimmy Christopher murmured: "Thank you, princess. What do you want me to do?"

"I want you to give up your senseless loyalty to a country that will be in slavery within twenty—four hours. Cast your lot with my father and with me. Montezuma will conquer the world—no power on earth can resist his exploding death. Montezuma the Third shall be Emperor of the World. You and I will be married in the temple of Huitzilopochtli, and Montezuma will make you the president of America. You will have more land to govern under my father than the president of the United States has; and you will have more power than any king. You will be a Prince of the Aztec Empire. And I will be your Princess!"

She stopped, breathing quickly, spasmodically, her eyes shining at the picture of power she had painted. She stepped back, drew herself up, displaying to the full the curves of her glorious figure. Her head, with its heavy knot of raven-black hair was held high on the white column of her throat, and she looked like some goddess of legend offering a chance at heaven to a mere mortal.

Jimmy Christopher gazed at her in frank admiration. His life had been a hard one, filled with action and the thunder of guns. He had found happiness and the zest of life in fighting for his country, and thoughts of women seldom interrupted the pattern of his existence except for the rare occasions when he saw Diane Elliot. Now this woman stood before him in all her beauty, in her sheer, ravishing loveliness.

He had to force himself to remember that it was this superbly beautiful woman who had caused a poor soldier to be tortured and then killed for failing to salute her. He had to force himself to remember that only a short while ago this deceptively handsome creature had ordered Diane Elliot to be placed upon the stone block of the altar in the sacrificial room, and had ordered that the heart be torn from Diane's living body as a sacrificial offering to a loathsome god.

And he said tightly, coldly: "Princess Dolores, you are a cruel, heartless beast. You have the body of a beautiful woman, but you have the mind and the soul of the Devil. I regret that I must refuse your kind offer."

For a moment the princess stared at him unbelievingly, as if she could not credit her ears. Then slowly her face became suffused with a deep, dull red. Her black eyes blazed with ungovernable rage, and her red lips twisted cruelly. She half crouched as if to leap at him, and her fingers bent, claw-like. A transformation took place, and Jimmy Christopher gazed at her in disgust. She was no longer beautiful.

For a moment, Jimmy Christopher thought that she would leap at him, with fingers clawed to rake the flesh from his face. But she mastered her rage, took a step toward the door. When she spoke, she was once more mistress of herself. She said, in a queer, low voice: "Then we shall see how a fool can die!"

She stood there for a long two minutes, staring at him, and a cunning look crept into her face. "Perhaps," she added enigmatically, "you shall have your satisfaction from Major Horgavo!"

Then she turned and walked from the cell, leaving Jimmy Christopher alone....

CHAPTER 11
THE DUEL

MINUTES PASSED, and no one entered the cell—minutes that seemed like hours to Jimmy Christopher, who knew that the time was so short to the moment when the exploding death would burst upon the soldiers congregating on the cliffs below.

He made futile attempts to release his wrists from those handcuffs, but to no avail. Doubt began to assail him there in the darkness of the cell—doubt as to whether or not his usually keen knowledge of human nature had failed him at this crucial moment. He had staked everything on the vanity that he had read in Horgavo's features. But if the major did not rise to the bait....

At last he heard footsteps outside, and the iron door creaked open. The two officers who had brought him here, entered. Their faces were grim, mask-like. They said nothing, but went about their work quickly.

One of them stepped close to Jimmy Christopher, grinned at him sneeringly, and unbuttoned Jimmy's coat and shirt. Then he stepped back, and the other produced a knife similar to those used by the priests.

Jimmy stared at him with narrowed eyes, thinking that they had come to murder him here in the cell. He tensed, prepared to defend himself with his feet.

But the officer had no intention of killing the prisoner. Instead, he seized Jimmy's coat and shirt in one hand, and slashed at them with the other. Two swift slashes on either side, and both coat and shirt came away in the officer's hand. Then the man with the knife seized Operator 5's undershirt, ripped it away viciously.

Jimmy's body was bared to the waist. The officer now stepped back, eyeing the smooth muscles of Jimmy's torso.

The second one now came closer, and ran his hands through the pockets of the prisoner's trousers, and transferred everything to his own pockets. A thick roll of bills that he found, he glanced at contemptuously, but kept.

Throughout the proceedings, not a single word was spoken.

Now, they released the handcuff which held Jimmy Christopher's left hand to the wall, and the officer with the knife clicked the cuff onto his own right wrist. Then the other officer did the same for Jimmy's right wrist, so that he stood between them, handcuffed to both men.

The officer with the knife had transferred it to his left hand, and he now held it's point to Jimmy Christopher's chest just below the heart, spoke for the first time:

"Come!" was all he said, in Spanish.

Out in the corridor was a file of soldiers, who fell in step behind them as they marched along the broad hall. Men turned to stare at the bare-torsoed prisoner under escort, and Jimmy saw that their glances were pitying.

The procession passed the open door of the room where the electronic rarefying device was located, and the white-smocked Maltbie came to the door to watch them pass. His restless eyes followed them until they turned a bend in the corridor.

Jimmy ventured a question to the one with the knife. "Would it be out of place for me to ask where we are going, señor?" he inquired courteously.

The other grunted, kept the point of his blade at Jimmy's chest, but made no response. Jimmy shivered a little. It was chilly going through the hall, with nothing to cover him from the waist up. He ventured once more: "Of course I realize, señor, that since I am only the principal in this ceremony, I have no business being curious. But I am dying to know where we are going."

The officer laughed harshly, and his knife point pricked the skin of Jimmy's chest. He winked across at his companion. "You are not dying—yet, Operator 5. But you will wish you were dying before the ceremony is over!" He continued to laugh, tickled at his conception of a witticism. Then, grudgingly, he added: "The Princess Dolores has decided that before you are turned over to the priests, you must give the satisfaction to the major Horgavo for the insult to him. You will fight him. He honors you by stooping to duel with you!"

JIMMY CHRISTOPHER'S blood raced. He had been right. His taunts had produced the proper effect. He was going to be permitted to duel with Horgavo!

The officer, watching him narrowly, said. "You are a fool. The major is a deadly swordsman. He will trim you down a bit for the amusement of the emperor and the princess—but he will be careful to leave enough for the priests to play with." He eyed Jimmy's muscular body appraisingly. "You are strong. You should last four or five days!"

Jimmy said courteously: "I hope you enjoy the spectacle, señor. I shall do my best to amuse you."

There was a flicker of admiration in the other's eyes, as he said to his companion on the other side of Jimmy: "This one is indeed a brave man. It is a pity that the princess hates him so. He must have said something terrible to her."

They passed through another wide corridor, and stopped before a closed door. Jimmy's keen eyes swept the hall, and he recognized the spot. This was the door to the sacrificial chamber from which he had fled only a little while ago, with Diane and his father. Now he was returning to it—a prisoner.

There were two guards standing before the door, and they opened it at once as Jimmy and his captors approached.

Jimmy passed inside between the two officers, leaving the file of soldiers outside. The door closed behind them.

The sacrificial chamber had been rearranged for the ceremony, whatever it was to be. On the altar still squatted the loathsome figure of the fat god, Huitzilopochtli. The bodies of the two priests whom Jimmy Christopher had killed were no longer there. But two other priests now stood before their god, with arms folded across their chests, glaring with fanatical eyes at their prospective victim.

Beside the altar had been erected a raised dais, and upon it now sat Montezuma, the Emperor of the Aztecs. He was attired in the full regalia of an Aztec emperor. Over his head hung a canopy skillfully wrought out of green feathers, gold and silver embroidery set with pearls. He wore a crown of gold on the front of which was emblazoned the figure of a bird of prey, the

Jimmy lunged, his blade flicking at the Emperor's unprotected face!

features of which were no less hawk-like than those of Montezuma himself. He was fully covered down to his wrists by a richly wrought suit of chain mail that fitted him like a glove. Over his shoulders was thrown carelessly a rich ermine cloak, and there were strings of pearls about his throat. He sat proudly erect, not even deigning to glance down at the room full of richly uniformed officers who thronged about the dais.

Beside him, on the right, on a lower chair, Jimmy Christopher saw the white, frightened face of Helen Powers. She, too, had been richly dressed, and she fidgeted nervously with a bit of her gown. Her eyes met those of Operator 5, and there was terrified, hopeless appeal in them.

Jimmy Christopher tried to look his reassurance at Helen Powers, and then switched his glance to the left of Montezuma, where sat the Princess Dolores.

She had changed her costume to one of brilliantly glittering white. Jewels adorned her white throat and her hands, and a long pin set with huge diamonds was thrust into the big black knot of hair at the nape of her neck.

Her black eyes gashed hate at Jimmy Christopher as he was led across the room.

In the center of the room Jimmy saw a peculiar wire cage. It was larger than those used for keeping prisoners—there was enough room in it for a dozen men to move about with ease. He was puzzled for an explanation of its presence, but that explanation was soon forthcoming.

The two officers did not lead him to the dais where Montezuma sat with his daughter and with Helen Powers. Instead they led him to this cage, turned a key in the lock of the wire door, and unfastened the handcuffs from his wrists. Then they thrust him into the cage, fastened the door.

JIMMY CHRISTOPHER turned coolly, surveyed the audience. They were all staring at him as some old Roman crowd might have stared at the gladiators in the arena, about to fight to the death for the delectation of the audience.

Montezuma touched a bell at the side of his seat, and the door at the side of the altar opened to admit Major Horgavo!

The major had removed his scarlet tunic, and he was in his shirtsleeves. He carried a naked sword in his right hand. He stepped with military precision up to the dais, bowed low, murmuring: "Lord, my lord, my great lord!"

Montezuma glanced at him, asked: "Are you ready, Horgavo?"

The major bowed low once more. "I am ready, mighty emperor!"

Montezuma smiled cruelly, turned to the cage in which Jimmy Christopher stood.

"Operator 5!" he said in ominous tones. "You have insulted an officer of the Aztec Empire. For that you must die. But before you die, you shall be taught humility. Major Horgavo has consented to fight a duel with you. Are you willing?"

Jimmy's glance met the gaze of the princess "I am willing," he said.

He was watching the princess. There seemed to be a queer quirk at her lips, as if she were enjoying a huge joke at his expense.

At a nod from Montezuma, Major Horgavo bowed, turned

and strode toward the cage. He was smiling cruelly, swinging his long sword ahead of him. The two officers at the door opened it, and Horgavo stepped inside the cage, stood facing Jimmy Christopher.

Now Jimmy saw that the men in the audience were all smiling broadly. There was some huge joke going on, of the nature of which he was not aware. He soon learned....

Montezuma, himself smiling wolfishly, ordered: "Let the prisoner be armed for the duel!" A page, who stood near the dais, now stepped forward, approached the cage. He was carrying a long wooden stick, perhaps an eighth of an inch in thickness, and about four feet long. He passed this in through the wires of the cage, offered it to Jimmy.

Operator 5 looked at the stick, and suddenly understood what they were all laughing at. This was not to be a duel. It was to be a cruel farce. He was to be compelled to face Horgavo, armed with a glittering steel sword; but he himself was to have no more than this stick.

He shrugged, took the stick. He hefted it in his hand, found that it weighed no more than about fifteen ounces. It would be no defense at all against the major's sword.

He smiled, bowed toward Montezuma's dais. But he addressed the princess. "Your highness is too generous!" he murmured.

Dolores was watching him with triumphant, malignant eyes. Montezuma raised and announced: "Major Horgavo will now give us a demonstration of accurate swordsmanship. It will be his task to slice off the prisoner's ears. He will do this, not with a single blow of his weapon, but only a bit at a time, until the prisoner's head has no further protuberances on either side. I have never liked the appearance of ears, and this will be an opportunity to see how a man looks without them."

His announcement was greeted with loud laughter from the uniformed officers, whose sadistic faces were lighted up with glee at the anticipation of the spectacle.

"The prisoner," Montezuma went on, "will, of course, be able to defend himself with his own weapon. Judging by his reputation he should put up a good fight."

Jimmy had been listening to Montezuma automatically. His eyes were on a small pile of articles that lay on the floor of the dais at Montezuma's feet. He recognized those articles. They were the things that Horgavo had taken from him in the cell. He distinguished his flat make-up case, his mechanical pencil, and three of the pencil bombs similar to the one he had used a while ago, except in color. The one he had used had been black. The others were green, red and yellow. There were also his file, and his compact tool kit, as well as many other items. Apparently Montezuma had been interested in the uses of the various things.

He was startled out of his study of the pile by the voice of the emperor. "Before the duel begins," the Aztec was saying, "it is only fitting that the noble fight which we are sure the prisoner will put up should be witnessed by some of his friends."

THE EMPEROR struck a bell twice, and the door at the side of the altar opened again. And an icy finger of despair coursed down Jimmy Christopher's spine. For there in the doorway, stood the two people for whose safety he had allowed himself to be dragged into this predicament. John Christopher and Diane Elliot were still prisoners!

Their hands were bound behind them, and they were urged into the room by a huge mestizo. Jimmy exclaimed huskily: "Diane! Dad!" His eyes blazed as he swung his gaze to the Princess Dolores. His lips formed a single word, which she heard distinctly: "Cheat!"

She flushed, half rose in her chair, then shrugged and subsided. Horgavo, watching Jimmy in the cage, chuckled. Diane cried out: "Jimmy! We couldn't leave you there, fighting, so we came back to look for you, to help you. And they caught us!"

Operator 5 groaned inwardly. "You—didn't deliver the warning?"

"No. We—"

Montezuma interrupted. He motioned to the mestizo, who pushed them forward until they were in front of the altar.

The emperor said to them: "You may watch your hero from there. No doubt you will be greatly entertained! After we are through with your hero, our priests will have some business with you both—on the altar!"

He clapped his hands twice. "Let the duel begin!"

Jimmy tore his eyes away from Diane and his father, swiveled to face Horgavo. The major was smiling, holding his sword over his heart, one hand on the hilt, the other fingering the sharp, pointed tip. He had his right leg slightly advanced, and his body leaned forward at the hips, in the position of the accomplished duelist.

He taunted Jimmy: "It is too bad that you have to be the

subject of my exhibition, Operator 5. Which ear shall I begin on—the right or the left?"

Christopher smiled at him bleakly. "Whichever you think you can reach first, major. For my part, I warn you that I shall aim for the heart!"

Horgavo laughed loudly at this, as did all the others in the room.

Diane wailed: "Jimmy! He'll kill you!"

And Operator 5 heard his father say: "Quiet, Diane! Jimmy knows what he's about!"

Then Horgavo took his fingers from the tip of the sword, let it whistle through the air in a vicious, glittering arc. Its edge came slashing down toward the side of Jimmy's head.

Jimmy swung his body an inch, brought up his stick, which he held like a sword. The two unequal weapons met in the air, and Horgavo's steel sliced through Jimmy's wood, shearing off a foot of it.

Horgavo stepped back quickly, executed a lightning-fast feint, then lunged. Jimmy Christopher fought calmly, his eyes locked with those of his adversary. He parried with all the skill in his possession, and the major frowned as his steel slithered off Jimmy's laughably short piece of wood without reaching its mark.

He couldn't understand how that maneuver had failed to bring the point of his sword to Jimmy's naked torso. It had been his intention to draw blood, then quickly to slash upward toward the ear. But he found his sword entangled by that short length of wood. Wherever he lunged, wherever he feinted, always his blade was met by the pitiable stick.

The throng in the room watched in silence, and the major grew more and more irritated. At last a vicious slash of his sword sheared off most of Jimmy's remaining stick. Jimmy stepped back quickly out of range, dropped the piece of wood remaining in his hand.

Horgavo smiled cruelly. "You put up a good fight. Operator 5. Now I will begin!"

He took a step forward, and Jimmy Christopher retreated before him. The major's eyes gleamed lustfully. From the dais, the princess cried out: "Go on, Horgavo. The exhibition! But remember—do not kill him yet!"

Jimmy had his back to the wire wall of the cages, eyes were still fixed on the major's, and his hand flew to the buckle of his belt. Horgavo advanced, his big white teeth showing as he smiled in triumph, his sword point extended toward Jimmy.

And suddenly Operator 5's hand flashed away from his belt. He had released the buckle, and the belt seemed to spring away from his body, to straighten out in his right hand. A flick of that hand, and the leather sheath fell away from the long, flashing rapier of Toledo steel that had rested within the belt.

Horgavo stopped, astounded, as the glittering steel flashed before his eyes in a bewildering series of lightning-fast thrusts. He parried the lunges mechanically, giving ground before the sudden furious onslaught of Jimmy's weapon.

Gasps of amazement went up from the audience. Montezuma shouted: "Quick! Open the cage and disarm him…!"

166

JIMMY CHRISTOPHER had taken the measure of Horgavo while he fought with the length of wood. Horgavo was an accomplished swordsman, but Operator 5 knew all the tricks that Horgavo knew, and then a few more. He forced the major back toward the door of the cage, and the major gave ground steadily. Perspiration covered his forehead, dripped down over his face. He understood that he had met his master, and sudden fear showed in his eyes.

He dared not take his glance from that bewilderingly swift blade of whistling steel that seemed to be everywhere at once. But he shouted in a panicky voice: "Quick! Help me!"

The two officers who stood near the door bustled frantically with the lock, got it open. But when one of them put out a hand to open the door and enter the cage, Jimmy's blade flicked out at him through the wire, pierced his wrist, then swung back to threaten the major.

The officer with the wounded wrist cried out in agony and jumped away. The second officer sprang toward the door, and once more Jimmy's rapier flicked out, this time through the muscles of the officer's arm. The man uttered a shriek of pain, fell back from the unlocked door.

Now Jimmy Christopher faced Horgavo. The man was sweating copiously, and he was so weary from the fast fighting that he could hardly lift his heavy sword.

Operator 5 said coldly: "I warned you, major—straight for the heart!" And his blade flashed swiftly through the air. "On guard, major!" he shouted. "Through the heart—in *tierce!*" His right knee bent, his wrist came up to a level with his shoulder, and he lunged!

Horgavo saw the point coming, and raised his sword for the parry. But his movements were like those depicted in a slow-motion camera beside Operator 5's Lightning lunge. Jimmy Christopher's point pierced the major's body right through the heart, and the heavy man dropped like a log.

Jimmy whipped his sword out of Horgavo's body, sprang backward and kicked open the door of the cage.

The room was in pandemonium, with a dozen men running toward the cage. Jimmy leaped across the floor, with men shouting behind him.

"Turn around, Dad!" he shouted, and John Christopher caught his meaning, spun around, extending his bound hands behind him.

Jimmy's sword flashed down swiftly, and the keen edge severed the cords that tied John Christopher's hands. Then Operator 5 leaped up on the dais, with men in uniform howling behind him. A revolver barked, then another. Lead flew through the room, whined and ricochetted. Jimmy glanced back to see that his father had picked up a revolver from one of the fallen men, and was pumping lead at the uniformed officers.

Operator 5 did not spare a second glance. He swung at Montezuma, who had arisen from his seat, dragging Helen Powers up in front of him. The emperor's face was ashen-white under his crown, and he twisted Helen Powers' arm behind her back, held her before him as a shield while he drew his own sword.

Jimmy glimpsed Dolores rushing at him, screaming wildly

168

above the thunder of the guns, her fingers curved to scratch like the claws of a wildcat. He sidestepped her, rushed at Montezuma.

Helen Powers' face was white with the pain of her twisted arm, as Montezuma backed away from the point of Jimmy's sword, dragging her with him.

Jimmy could not reach Montezuma without striking Helen Powers. The plucky little girl raised her foot, kicked back wildly. Her heel caught Montezuma in the shins, and he howled, relaxed his hold on her arm.

At once she dropped away, and Jimmy seized the opportunity. He stepped in quickly, his blade flicked out at the only spot in the emperor's body unprotected by chain mail—his face. Jimmy was grimly determined to kill. And kill he did. The point of his sword pierced through Montezuma's eye, and the emperor uttered a weird, ungodly shriek. Blood spurted gruesomely from the wound, and the emperor dropped to the floor of the dais, writhed there for a moment, shrieking. Then suddenly he stiffened, lay still. Jimmy's lunge had reached his brain.

Operator 5 swung from the dead body of the man who had planned to make America part of his empire, faced the brightly uniformed officers who had been storming the dais. John Christopher now had two guns in his hands, and both were blazing methodically. But he stopped as the officers suddenly fell back. They had seen their emperor killed. Some one among them began to shout: "Kill the gringos! They murdered Montezuma!" **JIMMY CHRISTOPHER** recognized the voice of Dolores, but he could not see her in the crowd of men. He did not wait for them to surge forward, but leaped from the dais, his sword point whirling before him. He reached quickly the small pile of his belongings on the dais, snatched up the three different-colored bombs in his hand.

"This way, Dad! Run, Diane! Run, Helen!" he shouted, and sprang toward the small door. John Christopher, Diane, and Helen Powers rushed to him, with the uniformed men after them.

But Jimmy had already pulled the pin from the green pencil-bomb. Now he flung it among the officers, and they leaped back from it, turned to flee the certain death they knew it would spew.

Jimmy tore open the door behind them, pushed his father and the two girls through just as the green pencil exploded with a terrific detonation that shook the rafters of the room.

Jimmy pulled the door closed, led the others through the room, over the planking that bridged the gap in the floor that his earlier bomb had left.

Behind them, on the other side of the door they heard the groans of dying men.

As they hurried out into the wide corridor, he said: "The green one was twenty percent stronger than the one I used before. This red one is fifty percent stronger, and the yellow one has almost the force of a Mills bomb. I'm going to use the yellow one now!"

The corridors were filled with armed men, with officers uttering hasty commands. Men were rushing to all the windows and doors, bringing up sub-machine guns. But they were paying no attention to Operator 5 and his companions.

Diane gasped, as she ran beside him: "Something's up, Jimmy!

These men don't even know what happened in the sacrificial room. Why are they hurrying?"

Operator 5 returned grimly: "Don't you hear it? There's musketry fire outside. Z-7's men are coming up!"

It was true enough. From outside came the rumble of rifle fire, the clatter of machine guns. The United States troops were attacking!

"Let's hurry," Jimmy urged, "before the exploding death goes into action!"

He left his father and Diane behind as he tore down the corridor to the room where he had seen Maltbie. The door was shut now, and he gripped the knob, twisted. It came open under his hand, and he saw the huge machinery of the exploding death in operation. The room was in darkness except for a glowing luminance tinged with all the colors of the spectrum, which came from the huge machine at the far wall. A dozen men were in the room now, stationed at various switches.

Maltbie himself was behind a huge metal desk, on which rested an instrument that resembled a compass. Operator 5 knew that this was the means of directing the electronic ray at whatever point on the map was desired.

Maltbie glanced up as the door opened, and his face twisted into a mask of fear as he saw Jimmy Christopher pulling the pin from the yellow pencil bomb.

His hand reached across the desk to snatch up a huge automatic that lay in front of him, and he leveled it at Operator 5. Jimmy Christopher did not move by so much as an inch from his position in the doorway. He was listening to the tick of his watch, counting. Even as Maltbie's finger contracted on the trigger of the automatic, Jimmy hurled his bomb into the room. Jimmy was deliberately throwing away his own life in order to wreck the exploding death device, in order to save the lives of those advancing United States troops outside....

But Maltbie never fired. For from behind Jimmy Christopher there came the wicked bark of an automatic; a slug whined past his ear, buried itself in Maltbie's heart. And Jimmy Christopher stepped quickly back, slammed the door on the terrific detonation that shook the whole building.

He turned, saw his father, still holding the automatic with which he had shot Maltbie over his son's shoulder. The two men looked at each other, and they smiled in understanding. These two made a remarkable fighting team.

Jimmy said simply: "Thanks, dad. That wasn't a split-second too soon!"

The door of the room behind them was creaking, yawing wildly open, sagging on broken hinges. Within, a fire was raging. The machinery had come tumbling down, had crashed through the floor. The body of Maltbie would never be recovered from the flaming inferno of that room. It had perished with the secret of his hellish device.

Diane Elliot, who, with Helen Powers, had panted up beside them, suddenly exclaimed exultantly: "Jimmy! They've broken through! Here come our men!"

From around the bend in the corridor came the staccato bursts of machine gun fire within the building. Men's screams sounded, and above all the noise and thunder rose the thrilling notes of a bugle!

AZTEC SOLDIERS came pouring back from the door, fleeing in panic. Jimmy and his father stood with guns in hand, with the girls behind them. But panic had seized the Aztec forces, with no one to command them. They fled pell-mell, passing right by the trio.

And in a moment, there appeared the bend of the corridor the familiar olive-drab of United States troops—with Z-7 in the lead beside a captain of infantry.

Z-7 raised a hand as he saw them, came running over with a glad shout. The troops poured by, rounding up the fleeing Aztecs. Z-7 clasped Jimmy's hand. "You've done it, boy. We climbed the cliffs unhindered! The exploding death—?"

Jimmy motioned toward the room behind them, where the fire was roaring, with flames licking out into the corridor. "There's the last of it, Z-7. It will never threaten the United States again!"

A small figure, fairly flying through the corridor, catapulted itself at Jimmy Christopher, threw arms about him.

Jimmy exclaimed gladly: "Tim! How are you, kid?"

Tim Donovan was speechless with joy. There were tears of gladness in his eyes. "Jimmy!" he finally managed to get out. "I—I never thought I'd see you alive again!"

They had moved down toward the door, away from the spreading heat of the fire. The infantry captain came up to them, saluted Z-7. "The Aztecs are completely routed, sir," he reported.

173

"Every last one of them killed or captured. I'm ordering the men out—this whole building will go up. Nothing can save it."

Z-7 nodded. Jimmy asked the captain: "Did you see any trace of a woman? Tall, dark, with black hair?"

The officer shook his head. "No sir. But as we were working up the cliff, we saw a helicopter take off from the roof of the house. Perhaps—"

Diane Elliot exclaimed: "She's escaped, Jimmy. I—I'm glad!"

Z-7 ordered a handsome young lieutenant to escort Helen Powers from the burning building—to take her back to her mother at the Beacon Hotel.

Outside, in the clearing, the olive drab soldiers herded their captives into a small circle, while the troops reformed.

Jimmy Christopher, Diane, John Christopher and Z-7 stood by themselves in a small group, watching the blaze. "There," Operator 5 said somberly, "is the funeral pile of the Aztec Empire."

The flames roared up into the night sky, throwing their sanguine blaze over the waters of the Hudson, clear across to the docks of New York on the other side. Suddenly the west wall crumbled, went toppling with the roar of thunder, down the cliffside. The heat from the flames became almost unbearable, and they were forced to move back. They watched while the rest of the old building caved in. As if by mutual agreement, no fire apparatus was sent for. It was as if they all wanted every last vestige of the ambitions of Montezuma to be consumed.

Finally Z-7 said: "Well, that's the end."

Jimmy Christopher shook his head. "I'm afraid not, Z-7."

The others looked at him questioningly. He explained. "While Dolores is still alive; the end is not here!"

Z-7 scoffed. "What! One woman! Tomorrow, when the rightful government of Mexico is restored to power, she will not even have a country! What can one woman do against the United States of America?"

Jimmy Christopher pressed the hand of Diane Elliot in the darkness. "I know that woman," he said somberly. "She is all evil, but she has supreme beauty, which is enough to turn men's heads. And I have seen how she can hate. I tell you, Z-7, that woman is dangerous!"

His eyes sought those of Diane. "Yet," he added in an undertone, "I can't feel sorry that she has escaped!" He felt Diane shudder beneath his arm as they turned to make their way down the cliff toward the river; toward a world of sanity again, and safety.

And somewhere in the void of the heavens a beautiful woman flew south; a woman whose full red lips were pressed into a tight, bitter line, and whose eyes behind the goggles were a terrible mirror of hate. Suddenly she turned around in the seat, and shouted into the void behind her: "We shall meet again, Operator 5. *We shall meet again....!*"

POPULAR HERO PULPS AVAILABLE NOW:

THE SPIDER
- ❏ #1: The Spider Strikes — $13.95
- ❏ #2: The Wheel of Death — $13.95
- ❏ #3: Wings of the Black Death — $13.95
- ❏ #4: City of Flaming Shadows — $13.95
- ❏ #5: Empire of Doom! — $13.95
- ❏ #6: Citadel of Hell — $13.95
- ❏ #7: The Serpent of Destruction — $13.95
- ❏ #8: The Mad Horde — $13.95
- ❏ #9: Satan's Death Blast — $13.95
- ❏ #10: The Corpse Cargo — $13.95
- ❏ #11: Prince of the Red Looters — $13.95
- ❏ #12: Reign of the Silver Terror — $13.95
- ❏ #13: Builders of the Dark Empire — $13.95
- ❏ #14: Death's Crimson Juggernaut — $13.95
- ❏ #15: The Red Death Rain — $13.95
- ❏ #16: The City Destroyer — $13.95
- ❏ #17: The Pain Emperor — $13.95
- ❏ #18: The Flame Master — $13.95
- ❏ #19: Slaves of the Crime Master — $13.95
- ❏ #20: Reign of the Death Fiddler — $13.95
- ❏ #21: Hordes of the Red Butcher — $13.95
- ❏ #22: Dragon Lord of the Underworld — $13.95
- ❏ #23: Master of the Death-Madness — $13.95
- ❏ #24: King of the Red Killers — $13.95
- ❏ #25: Overlord of the Damned — $13.95
- ❏ #26: Death Reign of the Vampire King — $13.95
- ❏ #27: Emperor of the Yellow Death — $13.95
- ❏ #28: The Mayor of Hell — $13.95
- ❏ #29: Slaves of the Murder Syndicate — $13.95
- ❏ #30: Green Globes of Death — $13.95
- ❏ #31: The Cholera King — $13.95
- ❏ #32: Slaves of the Dragon — $13.95
- ❏ #33: Legions of Madness — $12.95
- ❏ #34: Laboratory of the Damned — $12.95
- ❏ #35: Satan's Sightless Legion — $12.95
- ❏ #36: The Coming of the Terror — $12.95
- ❏ #37: The Devil's Death-Dwarfs — $12.95
- ❏ #38: City of Dreadful Night — $12.95
- ❏ ***NEW:*** #39: Reign of the Snake Men — $12.95

THE WESTERN RAIDER
- ❏ #1: Guns of the Damned — $13.95
- ❏ #2: The Hawk Rides Back from Death — $13.95

G-8 AND HIS BATTLE ACES
- ❏ #1: The Bat Staffel — $13.95

CAPTAIN SATAN
- ❏ #1: The Mask of the Damned — $13.95
- ❏ #2: Parole for the Dead — $13.95
- ❏ #3: The Dead Man Express — $13.95
- ❏ #4: A Ghost Rides the Dawn — $13.95
- ❏ #5: The Ambassador From Hell — $13.95

DR. YEN SIN
- ❏ #1: Mystery of the Dragon's Shadow — $12.95
- ❏ #2: Mystery of the Golden Skull — $12.95
- ❏ #3: Mystery of the Singing Mummies — $12.95

CAPTAIN ZERO
- ❏ #1: City of Deadly Sleep — $13.95
- ❏ #2: The Mark of Zero! — $13.95
- ❏ #3: The Golden Murder Syndicate — $13.95

Made in the USA
Middletown, DE
21 June 2023

33091338R00109